The *Tinkle* team had a tendency of changing office spaces every few years right from its time of inception. However, the office in Worli's Marthanda building would be the dearest since it is associated with a host of memories. This was where I first worked with Team *Tinkle* and where I first learnt that Mr. Pai could be quite like a school principal. 😃 Our stories and scripts submitted to him usually came back with remarks in red pen. If you were lucky, you would also get a 'Good' and that was something to be treasured.

Right from the beginning, the edit team of *Tinkle* has been known to be super noisy. Brainstorming funny characters, stories and scripts just means a lot of yakking. Plus, sharing quirky incidents, making fun of each other (*Tinkle* is a place where you do not grow up!), and pulling pranks just mean that we are basically a noise machine. Though Mr. Pai was known to be a strict disciplinarian in the 1980s, by the time my batch came along, he had mellowed. He would wryly request us to maintain some silence and decorum.

The edit team was also known to be made of major gluttons. So, since we were hungry all the time, we decided to start a hunger fund and stock one of the cabinets with biscuits and snacks. We got this big 'Snack Box' and filled it up with all sorts of goodies that were supposed to last us a week or even a fortnight. It lasted all of two days! 😃 And that was the end of the 'Snack Box'!

Did I mention that one of the favourite occupations of the team was to prank the unsuspecting? I was one such dupe and all Savio (Mascarenhas) had to tell me was that he lived in the outskirts of the city– a place so far away that he had to row a boat to reach home! Yup, I was gullible enough to swallow the tale and became the office laughing stock for weeks! However... I got my own back shortly and it was completely unplanned. In fact, Savio provided the fuel to his own fire.

You see, I had brought back some banana chips from Calicut. They were not only delicious but also did not leave oil stains when placed on tissue paper. Savio was so marvelled by these chips that he asked me how they were made. Now if someone was so intent on digging their own grave, why shouldn't I provide the shovel? I innocently told him that the chips were fried in water. Savio looked so stunned and delighted with my answer. He said, 'Wow! Really?' Of course, snickers followed Savio wherever he went for the next few weeks. 😃

Memories come, memories go but as you turn these pages, I hope they help you recollect your favourite memories with *Tinkle*. I also hope you help in making new *Tinkle* memories.

Happy reading,
Rajani Thindiath
Editor-in-Chief, *Tinkle*

EDITOR-IN-CHIEF : RAJANI THINDIATH
GROUP ART DIRECTOR : SAVIO MASCARENHAS
EDITORIAL TEAM : SEAN D'MELLO, APARNA SUNDARESAN, RITU MAHIMKAR, AASHLINE ROSE AVARACHAN, JUBEL D'CRUZ, POOJA WAGHELA
HEAD OF CREATIVE SERVICES : KURIAKOSE SAJU VAISIAN
DESIGN TEAM : TARUN SOMANATHAN, KETAN TONDWALKAR
COVER DESIGN : AKSHAY KHADILKAR

ISBN 978-93-88957-14-4
Published by Amar Chitra Katha Pvt. Ltd., 7th Floor, AFL House, Lok Bharati Complex,
Marol Maroshi Road, Andheri (East), Mumbai – 400059, India
Tel: +91 22 4918 888 1/2
www.tinkle.in | www.amarchitrakatha.com
Printed in India

Get in touch with us:

tinklemail@ack-media.com
@TinkleMagazine
Tinkle Comics Studio
@tinklecomicsstudio
www.tinkleonline.com
www.amarchitrakatha.com
www.tinkle.in
Amar Chitra Katha Pvt.Ltd, 7th floor, AFL House, Lok Bharati Complex, Marol Maroshi Road, Andheri (East), Mumbai 400059

Readers' Choice

A PAIR OF CUCKOOS

Illustrations : Ram Waeerkar

Based on a story sent by Praveen Kirpalani, Bombay

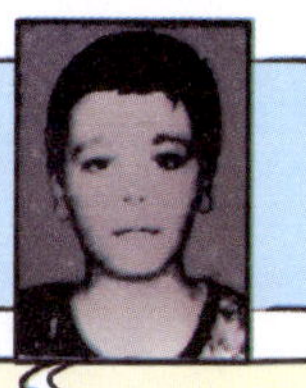

THE MARVELLOUS MELON

Illustrations : V.B. Halbe

READERS' CHOICE

Based on a story sent by Zakir Ali, Jodhpur

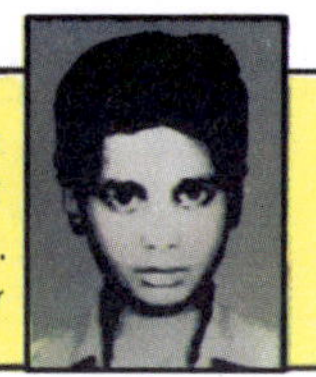

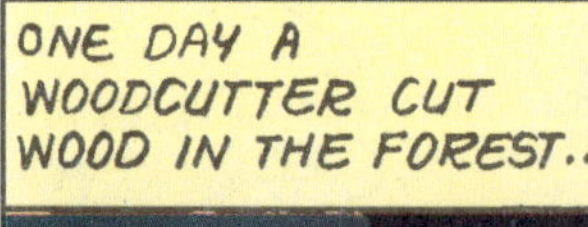

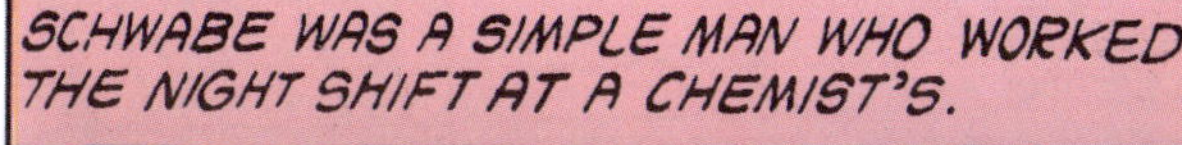

AN INTERESTING FEATURE ABOUT THE SUN IS SUNSPOTS. THESE ARE DARK SPOTS WHICH APPEAR ON THE BRIGHT SURFACE OF THE SUN AND MOVE AND DISAPPEAR AFTER SEVERAL DAYS. THESE SPOTS ARE ACTUALLY AREAS WHERE THE SUN'S SURFACE IS SLIGHTLY COOLER THAN NORMAL: ABOUT 4000°C INSTEAD OF 6000°C.

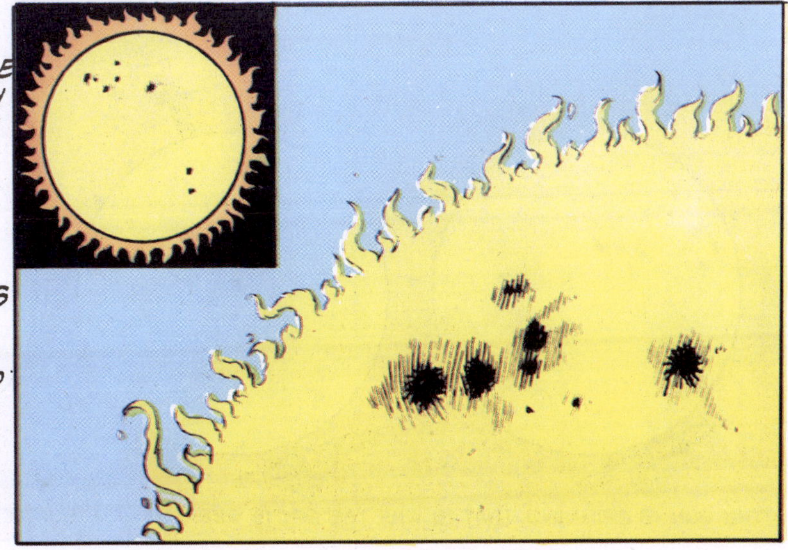

SCHWABE STARTED STUDYING THESE SUNSPOTS. HE KEPT A RECORD OF HOW MANY SUNSPOTS HE SAW EVERYTIME HE LOOKED AT THE SUN.
DURING SOME YEARS HE SAW VERY FEW SPOTS, DURING OTHERS HE SAW SEVERAL. HE FOUND THAT THE GREATEST NUMBER OF SUNSPOTS COULD BE SEEN EVERY ELEVEN YEARS. THIS DISCOVERY WAS OF GREAT IMPORTANCE TO ASTRONOMERS.

BUT SUNSPOTS CERTAINLY HELPED SCIENTISTS TO LEARN SOMETHING ABOUT THE SUN. BY WATCHING THE POSITIONS OF THE SUNSPOTS ON THE SURFACE OF THE SUN, THEY FOUND OUT THAT THE SUN SPINS ON ITS AXIS.

Nasruddin Hodja

Script : Shruti Desai
Illustrations : Ram Waeerkar

RESULTS OF THE COMPLETE--THE-STORY COMPETITION NO 7*

Most of our TINKLE readers must have been very busy with their exams, because we received fewer entries this time than ever before! However, three entries were found eminently suitable for prizes.

Ehpriya Matharu
C/o. H. S. Matharu
P. O. Box 57359
Nairobi, Kenya.

Shridhar Shivaramu and **S. Krishna Dass** both of Bangalore, have each been awarded a consolation prize of Rs. 25

The Prize-winning entry:

The people started to chase the jeep and managed to stop it. The monkey jumped out and ran through the crowd, back to the circus tent. It took off its face mask and its furry costume and VOILA! It was a man!

The man performed a juggling act and then began to throw pies at the other animals. The crowd realized that the man was a clown and this was all part of the act!

* Refer to the footnote under the Editor's Note

THE VALUE OF TIME

Illustrations : Ashok Dongre

Readers' Choice

Based on a story sent by Hemendra Kumar, Ujjain

A MAN ONCE WENT TO SEE THE KING.

THE HAPPY MAN RUSHED HOME.
WIFE! THE KING HAS GIVEN ME PERMISSION TO TAKE AS MUCH MONEY AS I WANT FROM THE TREASURY.

EEEE-WOW!

TAKE ALL THESE BAGS! YOU MUST BRING AS MUCH MONEY AS YOU CAN.
FOOLISH WOMAN FIRST GIVE ME SOME FOOD.

HOW DO YOU EXPECT ME TO LIFT THE BAGS ON AN EMPTY STOMACH?
AH...YES, YES!

THE MAN ATE HIS FILL...

...AND SET OUT–
OH, IT IS SO HOT! WHY DON'T I REST FOR A WHILE...

...JUST A LITTLE WHILE!

SOON–
ZZZZZZ!

AFTER SOME TIME–
OH...OH! I'VE OVERSLEPT

ANYWAY, THERE'S ENOUGH TIME FOR ME TO GET TO THE PALACE BEFORE SUNDOWN.

AS HE WALKED FURTHER...
I WONDER WHAT'S GOING ON HERE?

AN ACROBAT, PERFORMING TRICKS...

...THE SUN IS STILL UP. I'LL WATCH FOR A WHILE!

JUST A LITTLE WHILE!

ONE HOUR LATER —
OH... OH... THE SUN IS ABOUT TO SET... I'D BETTER HURRY.

HE RAN AS FAST AS HE COULD.

WAIT! WAIT!

CLANG!

IT'S NOT A FALSE RUMOUR THEN. YOU DO HAVE THE HABIT OF BEING LATE.

ANYWAY, YOU'VE JUST LOST A FORTUNE BECAUSE OF IT.

THE CITY LOVER

READERS' CHOICE

Based on a story sent by Hemal Parikh
Illustrations: Ram Waeerkar

Kalia
THE CROW
Script:
LUIS
Illustrations:
RAM WAEERKAR

THE JUNGLE IS OUR HOME...

...AND WE SHOULD MAKE IT SAFER FOR EVERYBODY.
SAFER! IT'S TOO SAFE FOR SOME ANIMALS ALREADY.

I HAVEN'T CAUGHT A RABBIT IN MONTHS.
ER... CHAMATAKA...

DID YOU RAID BABLOO'S CAVE TODAY?
YES... BUT ALL I GOT WAS HALF A HONEYCOMB.

WELL, HE'S COMING HERE.
WHAT?

LET'S GET OUT OF HERE.
HEY, WAIT.

...NOW WHO'LL LOOK AFTER THE BRIDGES?
WE WILL!

THIS IS AMAZING!
WE'LL GET TO WORK AT ONCE. COME ON, DOOB DOOB.

WHEW! THAT WAS CLOSE!
CHAMATAKA, THERE'S A BRIDGE AHEAD.

IT'S HOLLOW.
HOLLOW?

WHAT A DELIGHTFUL BRIDGE!

TRY TO GO ACROSS IT NOW.

SPLSH!

WAIT THERE...

...AND I'LL THROW SOME ANIMAL DOWN FOR YOU IN THE SAME WAY.
ALL RIGHT.

IS THAT THE LOG, KALIA?
YES!
?

IT'S ROTTEN. IT'S NOT SAFE FOR ANYONE TO CROSS OVER IT.

KER-PLOSH!

YOU WERE RIGHT. THAT LOG WASN'T SAFE.

IT'S EVEN MORE DANGEROUS THAN I THOUGHT.
LET GO! IT'S ME, YOU IDIOT!

It's magic!

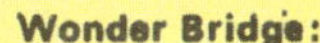

Wonder Bridge:

Challenge someone to make a piece of paper support a glass atop two spaced glasses.

Secret:

Fold the paper concertina-wise. It's strong enough to carry the glass!

Disappearing Pencil:

Place a pencil under a handkerchief. Toss the handkerchief aside and the pencil is gone!!

Secret:

As soon as you've placed the pencil under the handkerchief, extend your fore-finger to make it appear to be the pencil holding up the handkerchief.

At the same time, drop the pencil down your sleeve. When the handkerchief is removed, the pencil is gone! Remember, magic means practice and practice builds your confidence in the art of magic.

4 Coins to 5:

Set up four coins on a table in front of you. Count them off so that there can be no mistake about the fact that there are only four coins on the table.

Now slide these coins off the table and — voilà — you have five!

Secret:

Under the table there is a fifth coin which you have attached with a piece of soap. While you are gathering the four coins from the table top, simply reach under the table with your fingers, palming the fifth coin. A neat trick.

Amaze and astonish your friends with these astounding tricks. Easy to do but hard to believe.

And here's a trick that's most simple to do. Open a State Bank Savings Account in your name. If you are below 10, ask Daddy to open an Account for you. Put in your pocket money. And all the gift money you receive. And then watch your savings double and even treble as you grow.

Saving can be fun!

Security is a warm feeling

* Refer to the footnote under the Editor's Note

TANTRI THE MANTRI

Script: Appaswami
Illustrations : Ashok Dongre

...BUT IT CAN'T LAND. I'VE YET TO FIX THE LANDING KEY.

A HORSE THAT FLIES BUT CANNOT LAND...

HERE IS A THOUSAND RUPEES.

I'LL TAKE THE HORSE!

BUT SIR, THE WORK IS INCOMPLETE.
THAT DOESN'T MATTER.

I'LL SEND HOOJA THE RAJA FLYING...

...AND I'LL TAKE HIS PLACE ON THE THRONE! HEH-HEH!

MAHARAJ!

I'VE BROUGHT YOU A FLYING HORSE!
A FLYING HORSE!

COME, FLY!
NOT NOW, TANTRI. I HAD A HEAVY BREAKFAST.

WONDERFUL! YOU SHOULD NEVER FLY ON AN EMPTY STOMACH.

COME WITH ME!

TURN THE KEY...

I CAN'T LEAVE WITHOUT THE ROYAL UMBRELLA.
HURRY UP WITH THAT UMBRELLA!

HURRY! HURRY!

NOW TURN THE KEY... KEY...

YAHOO!

HE'S GONE!

NOW I'LL BE THE RAJA!

SIR!
?

YOU?
WOULD YOU LIKE TO BUY THIS?

WHAT IS THIS?

IT IS CALLED...

OUCH!
CRASH

... A MAGNET. IT'S A VERY POWERFUL MAGNET.
CLUNK!

LATER—
I ENJOYED THE FLIGHT TANTRI...

... BUT THE LANDING WAS A LITTLE UNCOMFORTABLE.

THE LOTUS
Our National Flower
Script :
Prof (Mrs.) S.M. Almeida
Illustrations :
J.P. Irani
THE LOTUS GROWS IN SWEET, SHALLOW AND STAGNANT WATER.
THE FLOWERS ARE SCENTED. THEY OPEN AT SUNRISE AND CLOSE IN THE AFTERNOON.
THEY STAND ERECT ON LONG STALKS ABOVE THE WATER LEVEL.
THE LEAVES ARE LARGE, DARK GREEN AND SHINY.
THEIR UPPER SURFACE HAS A WAXY COATING.
WATER FALLING ON THE LEAVES RUNS OFF LIKE SILVERY WHITE DEW-DROPS.
STRONG VEINS ON THEIR LOWER SURFACE HELP THEM TO STAY IN POSITION AND WITHSTAND WATER CURRENTS.
VEINS

THE STEM OF THE LOTUS LIES BURIED IN THE MUD OF THE LAKE OR POND. IT IS A CREEPING STEM AND IT LIES HORIZONTALLY UNDER THE MUD. SPONGY ROOTS GROW OUT FROM IT. THE ROOTS FIX THE PLANT FIRMLY IN THE SOIL AND ALSO SUCK UP NOURISHMENT FROM IT.

A NEW PLANT CAN GROW FROM A PIECE OF THE STEM.

THE STEM ITSELF IS SWOLLEN WITH FOOD MATERIAL. THE FOOD MATERIAL IS STORED IN THE FORM OF STARCH.

THE STEM IS USED AS A VEGETABLE. IT HAS MEDICINAL USES TOO.

THE FRUIT OF THE LOTUS TOO, CAN BE EATEN.

THE LOTUS SEED HAS A THIN BUT HARD SHELL. THE ALMOND-COLOURED KERNEL IS NUTRITIOUS. THE GREEN DORMANT BUD IS BITTER AND MUST BE REMOVED BEFORE EATNG.

THE WATER LILY

UNLIKE THE LEAVES OF THE LOTUS WHICH STAND ABOVE THE SURFACE OF THE WATER, THE LEAVES OF THE WATER LILY FLOAT ON THE WATER.

READERS' CHOICE

HOW THE GIRAFFE GOT HIS LONG NECK

Illustrations : Ashok Dongre

Based on a story sent by Mahul V. Desai, Bombay

...THE OSTRICH HID BEHIND SOME BUSHES...

...BUT, THE GIRAFFE, HAVING NO PLACE TO HIDE...

...PUT HIS NECK INTO THE HOLLOW OF A TREE.

AFTER SOMETIME—
I SPY GIRAFFE...!

HELP!
?!

WHAT'S THE MATTER?
I'M STUCK.

?
DON'T WORRY! I'LL PULL YOU OUT.

GIVE ME A HAND!

SOON ALL THE OTHER ANIMALS CAME TO HELP...

... AND ALL OF THEM BEGAN TO PULL.

THEY PULLED AND PULLED.

AND IN THE END—
POP

?!

DON'T WORRY! A LONG NECK IS VERY USEFUL ... I SHOULD KNOW.

THERE, WHAT DID I TELL YOU. YOU WOULD NEVER HAVE REACHED THOSE LEAVES EARLIER.
YOU'RE RIGHT.

GIRAFFES EVER SINCE HAVE HAD LONG NECKS.

FLOWERS FOR A PEN

Illustrations : Dilip Kadam

Based on a story sent by
M.S. Chakravarthy
Chikballapur

EDITOR'S CHOICE

My young friends,

Long ago, there lived a poor woman in a village near Mysore. She worked very hard and saved enough money to buy two gold bangles. She wanted everyone to admire her new bangles, but no one paid any attention to them. This worried her. She desperately wanted her bangles to be noticed.

So one day she set fire to her hut and began to cry for help, waving her wrists wildly in the air. People came running to help put out the fire. But no one so much as glanced at her bangles.

The fire reduced her hut and everything in it to ashes.

The woman had to sell the bangles to build a new hut and to buy new clothes and other necessities.

This story was sent by R. Rakesh of Bangalore.

Affectionately yours,

Uncle Pai

Mooshik

Based on an idea suggested by Jairaj Sounderrajan, Bombay

Readers Write...

The spider saved the prince's life in the story, "A Friend in Need" which you featured in TINKLE No. 43. But how did the prince get out of the cave? He wouldn't harm his little friend by breaking the cobweb, would he?

Monica Phanse
Bombay

I am delighted with the new series of animal stickers. But in future, instead of animals, why don't you give us stickers of stars, rockets; different types of aeroplanes, cars and steamers?

Lalit Dabholkar
Bombay

I'm very glad that you have started the "Say it Yourself" contest. But please make sure that the entry form does not appear behind animal life or an interesting story.

Syed Sakkaf
Bhatkal

I am a regular reader of TINKLE, but it comes very late to Hyderabad. "The Stone Soup" in TINKLE No. 43 was very interesting. Please publish more stories like this.

T. S. Phani
Hyderabad

During my vacations I always go to my village and I carry along several copies of TINKLE so that my friends there can also enjoy TINKLE as much as I do!

Arif Bankotkar
Bombay

CUT HERE

ENTRY FORM*

Say it Yourself – 7

NAME ____________________

ADDRESS ____________________

____

____

STATE ____________________

PIN ____________________ ☐☐☐☐☐☐

Answer: ____________________

____

____

____

____

____

* Refer to the footnote under the Editor's Note

ANWAR
by
Appaswami
Illustrations: V. B. Halbe

WHAT ARE YOU DOING? HAVE YOU FINISHED YOUR HOMEWORK?
I WANT TO PLAY, AMMA.

ALL RIGHT, WE WILL PLAY....
BUT HIS HOME-WORK....

LEAVE IT TO ME.

LET'S PLAY 'SCHOOL.'
SCHOOL?

YES, YOU BE THE TEACHER. WE ARE THE STUDENTS.
TEACH US HOW TO WRITE A B C....

I'M THE TEACHER....
YES, SIR.

YOU WILL DO AS I SAY....
YES, SIR.

NOW PLEASE SHOW US HOW TO....
WAIT!

TODAY IS A HOLIDAY! GO OUT AND PLAY.
!!

NO. 50

Rs. 3

TINKLE

THE FORTNIGHTLY FOR CHILDREN FROM THE HOUSE OF AMAR CHITRA KATHA

THE FISHERMAN AND HIS DAUGHTERS

MEET THE EARTHWORM

PRASAD IYER

The profilic writer and artist, Mr. Prasad Iyer, started his time at *Amar Chitra Katha* as a production assistant. Though writing wasn't a part of his job, he had a knack for it and soon started writing for *Tinkle*. But Mr. Iyer wasn't merely content with writing; he also learnt how to draw. And soon he became one of the few people who both wrote and illustrated their stories.

The first *Tinkle* Toon he illustrated was Kalia the Crow. Apart from Kalia, he often wrote scripts for other *Tinkle* Toons such as Shikari Shambu, Tantri, Suppandi and Nasruddin Hodja. Some of the more memorable *Tinkle* stories such as 'The Pawned Sword' and 'A Short Man's Dilemma' were scripted by Mr. Iyer.

Mr. Iyer had come to writing from a science background. This enabled him to make his mark while writing tons of science features and science fiction stories. His features made concepts like pressure and optical illusions easy to understand.

There was a time when the first *Tinkle* team had moved on. Mr Iyer helped Mr. Pai (co-founder and founding editor) keep the magazine running during those difficult times. Later, he developed an interest in researching and writing comics based on the army. He was fascinated by India's military history. He created some of these for *Tinkle*, one of which was 'Voyage of the "Trishna"', based on the INS Trishna, the first sailboat from India to circumnavigate the Earth.

SAY IT YOURSELF AND WIN A CASH PRIZE* NO.7

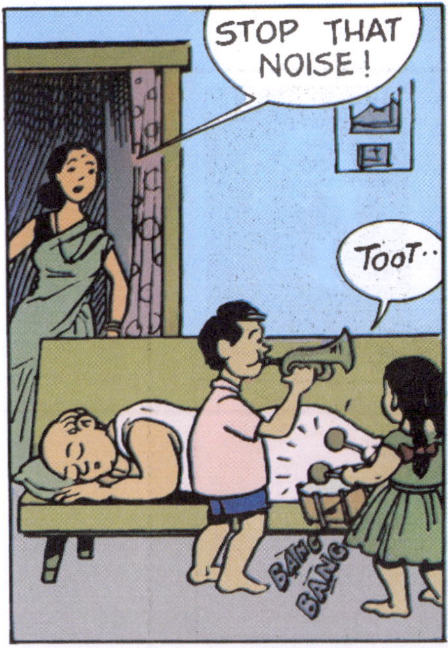

1. Mail your entry to:
   TINKLE Competition Section,
   P. Bag No. 16541 Bombay 400026
2. • First prize - Rs. 50/- • Second prize - Rs. 25/-
   • Third prize - Rs. 15 - • 10 Consolation prizes, - Rs. 10/- each
3. Decision of the judges is final and binding. Names of the prize-winners will be announced in TINKLE No. 55
4. Entry form for Say It Yourself No. 7 is given on page No. 14

Last date for receiving entries: 10.2.1984

Winners of 'Say it Yourself'* No. 5

FIRST PRIZE (Rs. 50)	SECOND PRIZE (Rs. 25)	THIRD PRIZE (Rs. 15)
N. Shanti Kumar 33 60 Ramakrishna-puram, Secunderabad 500556	**Syed Azher Ali** C o Syed Mehdi Ali 11-4-654 Saifabad Hyderabad 500004	**Vinayak N. Bankapur** C o. N.R. Bankapur Housing Colony C-7 Bagalkot, Dist. Bijapur 587101

Consolation Prizes of Rs. 10 each

Sriram B. Bangalore 560010

K. Vasuki Bangalore 560078

Dhyana R. Shobha Bangalore 560011

Padmakar J. Thomas Thana 401504

Gayatri Patel Bombay 400025

Vikram Somani Bombay 400020

P. Renuka Ganapathy Mysore 570002

Rashi Koul Srinagar 190001

S. Deepti Bangalore 560003

Neetu Punjabi Bombay 400052

Prize-winning entry from N. Shanti Kumar

* Refer to the footnote under the Editor's Note

DID YOU KNOW?

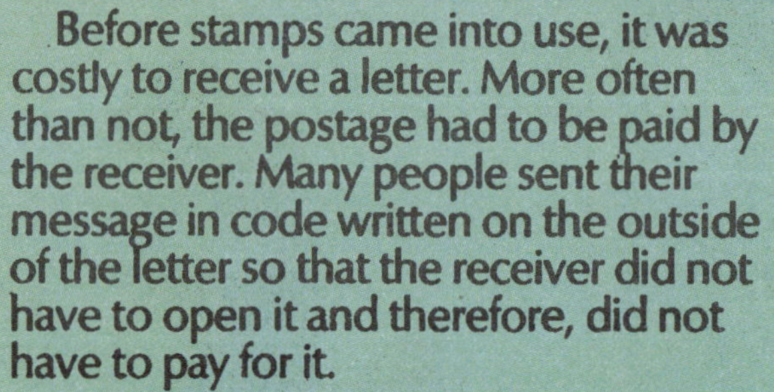

Before stamps came into use, it was costly to receive a letter. More often than not, the postage had to be paid by the receiver. Many people sent their message in code written on the outside of the letter so that the receiver did not have to open it and therefore, did not have to pay for it.

Penny Black

The first postage stamp of the world, the 'Penny Black' was issued in Great Britain on May 6, 1840.

Indian stamp of 1854

The first postage stamps for general use all over India were issued on July 1, 1854. The stamps were in denominations of half an anna. one anna, two annas and four annas and portrayed Queen Victoria of England.

Till 1926, Indian stamps were printed in London. Then it became the responsibility of the India Security Press, Nasik.

Writing in Ancient India

Script: Subba Rao Illustrations: Anand Mande

THE LEAF OR THE BARK, AS THE CASE MAY BE, WAS DRIED, SMOOTHED AND CUT INTO STRIPS.

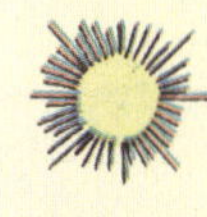

A BOOK CONSISTED OF SEVERAL SUCH STRIPS HELD LOOSELY TOGETHER BY EITHER A SINGLE CORD PASSED THROUGH A HOLE IN THE CENTRE OR BY TWO CORDS AT EITHER END.

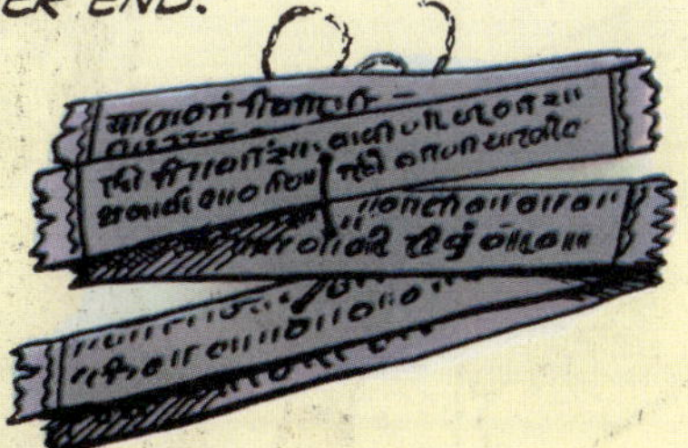

THE BOOKS HAD HARD WOODEN COVERS WHICH WERE OFTEN PAINTED.

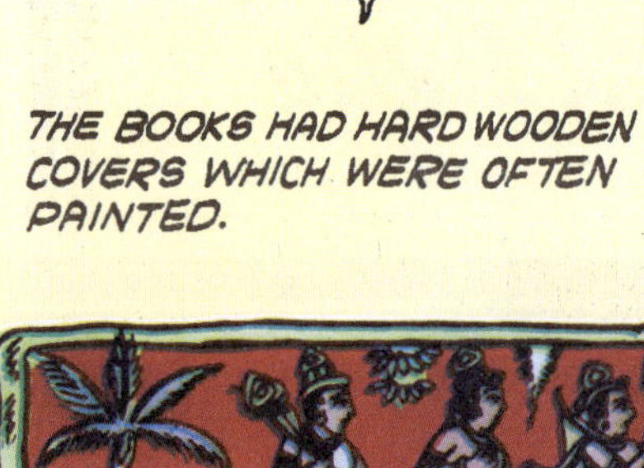

THE INK WAS MADE FROM LAMP BLACK OR CHARCOAL, APPLIED WITH A REED PEN.

SOMETIMES, THE LETTERS WERE SCRATCHED ON THE PALM-LEAF WITH A STYLUS...

...AND FINELY POWDERED LAMP BLACK OR CHARCOAL WOULD BE SPRINKLED ON THE LEAF.

LATER THE EXCESS POWDER WOULD BE BLOWN AWAY...

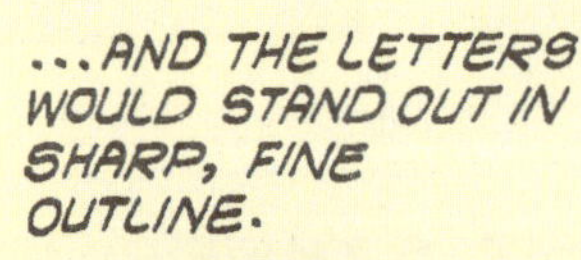

...AND THE LETTERS WOULD STAND OUT IN SHARP, FINE OUTLINE.

IMPORTANT DOCUMENTS WERE ENGRAVED ON COPPER PLATES.

THE THIEF

Illustrations :
Ram Waeerkar

Readers' Choice

Based on
a story sent
by Kado,
Bhutan

THE HOURS PASSED...
YAWN..NN

ZZZZZZZZZZZZZ
...AND BOTH FELL ASLEEP.

SUDDENLY—
THUD
EH!

THE THIEF!

YOU RASCAL!
THOP! THOP!
STOP! STOP!

IT'S ME!
ME? WHO?

BADDU! SO YOU'VE BEEN STEALING THE MANGOES!
DON'T BE STUPID...

...I FELL OFF THE TREE.
OH!

YOU KNOW, WHILE I WAS UP THERE I SAW THE BUNCH OF MANGOES WHICH I THOUGHT WAS MISSING.

I WAS LOOKING AT THE WRONG BRANCH.
ME TOO.

THERE ARE THE TWO MANGOES WHICH I THOUGHT HAD BEEN STOLEN.

WE HAVE WASTED OUR TIME! LET'S GO IN AND GET SOME SLEEP.
YES!

OUR HOUSE! OUR HOUSE HAS BEEN STOLEN!
OH, MY GOD!

WHAT SHALL WE DO NOW?
?

OH, IT'S ON THAT SIDE!
WHAT A RELIEF!

THE BROTHERS RUSHED IN AND WENT TO BED.

GREEN GOLD
Illustrations : Dilip Kadam
Based on a story sent by
Eren Rosario, Goa
Readers' Choice
BEHNJI...
GIVE ME TEN PAISE, BEHNJI...
TEN PAISE? NO! I'LL GIVE HER SOMETHING ELSE.

I WON'T GIVE YOU MONEY...TAKE THESE PLANTS INSTEAD.

GROW THEM WITH CARE, AND YOU WILL BE REPAID A HUNDRED-FOLD!

WHEN THE BEGGAR GIRL REACHED HER HOME...
THERE YOU ARE, CHAMPA! HOW MUCH DID YOU GET TODAY?
MOTHER, I HAD NO LUCK TODAY. A GIRL GAVE ME SOME PLANTS AND THAT'S ALL I GOT.

PLANTS? THEY ARE OF NO USE!

I AM SURE THE GIRL MEANT WELL. I'LL GIVE THESE PLANTS ALL MY LOVE AND CARE.

CHAMPA PLANTED THE SAPLINGS...

...AND TENDED THEM WITH LOVING CARE. A FEW DAYS LATER—
HOW WELL THEY ARE GROWING.

CHAMPA BEGAN TO SPEND A GREAT DEAL OF TIME WITH HER PLANTS...
...AND GRADUALLY, INSTEAD OF GOING OUT TO BEG FOR MONEY...

...SHE BEGAN TO ASK AROUND FOR SEEDS AND SAPLINGS.

VERY SOON FLOWERS OF ALL SORTS BEGAN TO BLOOM IN HER BACKYARD.
WHAT A PRETTY GARDEN.

WILL YOU SELL ME SOME ROSES?
CERTAINLY.

AND I WOULD LIKE SOME ASTERS.

MOTHER, SEE WE DON'T HAVE TO BEG ANYMORE. WE CAN GROW FLOWERS AND VEGETABLES AND SELL THEM...
YOU'RE RIGHT.

I'LL GET SOME MANURE.

HEY, WHERE ARE YOU GOING WITH THOSE FLOWERS?

THEY'RE FOR THE LADY WHO GOT ME STARTED ON ALL THIS, MOTHER.

GOOD ADVICE

A Nasruddin Hodja tale **Illustrations : Ram Waeerkar**

Readers' Choice

Based on a story sent by V. Nagarik, Hyderabad

SECONDLY, DON'T EVER BELIEVE THAT FLAMES OF FIRE CAN BECOME HARD OR SOLID.
!

AND LASTLY, DON'T EVER BELIEVE THAT ICE CAN BE HOT.
WHAT NONSENSE ARE YOU SPOUTING?

I DON'T WANT YOUR 'WISE SAYINGS'! GIVE ME MONEY INSTEAD.
TOO LATE! YOU ASKED FOR THE SAYINGS.

PLACE THE BASKET NEAR THE WINDOW.

!

WHY DID YOU THROW IT OUT?
YOU TOLD ME TO PLACE IT NEAR THE WINDOW.

HOW SHOULD I KNOW WHETHER YOU MEANT INSIDE OR OUTSIDE THE ROOM?

AND IF ANYONE TELLS YOU THERE'S A SINGLE BOTTLE UNBROKEN IN THAT BASKET...

...DON'T BELIEVE HIM!

Kalia
THE CROW
Script:
LUIS
Illustrations :
RAM-WAEERKAR

MY THROAT IS PARCHED AH, A WATERHOLE!

GLUG-GLUG-GLUG

?
WHAT'S HAPPENED TO HIM?

GLUG
GLUG
GLUG

THAT WATER WEAKENS ANYONE WHO DRINKS IT!

IF LIONS AND ELEPHANTS STAGGER AFTER DRINKING IT, YOU CAN IMAGINE WHAT IT WOULD DO TO SMALLER ANIMALS!

THEY WON'T BE ABLE TO RUN AWAY... HEE HEE HEE!

DOOB DOOB! YOU HIDE IN THOSE BUSHES...

I'LL FIND A THIRSTY DEER AND BRING IT HERE.
ALL RIGHT!

THIS IS OUR LUCKY DAY!

OOOPS... KALIA! THAT CROW COULD UPSET ALL OUR PLANS!

HEY, WHY DON'T I GET RID OF THAT BIRD FIRST!

ER... KALIA, YOU LOOK THIRSTY.
I'M NOT.

BUT YOU'LL SOON BE... THERE'S A WATERHOLE NEARBY WHERE THE WATER IS AS SWEET AS HONEY.
YOU DON'T SAY!

COME AND SEE FOR YOURSELF!
I'M SURE IT'S A TRAP...

...BUT I'LL GO ALONG.

THERE'S THE WATERHOLE.

FLY DOWN AND HAVE A SIP.
A SIP SHOULD BE ENOUGH FOR HIM.... HEE HEE HEE.

CHAMATAKA HAS BROUGHT KALIA... WONDERFUL!

WE'LL GET RID OF THAT MEDDLESOME CROW FIRST!

GO ON DRINK!
HE'S NOT DRINKING!

HE SUSPECTS SOMETHING... I'LL RUSH OUT AND GRAB HIM.

?!
WHAT THE...!

SPLOSH!
—AAAH... (GLUG) ... (GLUG)...

DRAT! I MISSED!

BUT WHAT'S HAPPENED TO CHAMATAKA!

CHAMATAKA, HEY CHAMATAKA! ARE YOU ALL RIGHT?
PERHAPS THE WATER WAS TOO SWEET FOR HIM!

ADVENTURES OF A SON-IN-LAW

Script: Meera Ugra
Illustrations: Ram Waeerkar

THUD

OH, GOD! I HAVE FALLEN INTO A GRAIN-PIT!

?
SOMEBODY'S COMING.

MASTRAM!
OH, IT'S MY BROTHER-IN-LAW!

HELP ME UP.

I...ER... WENT DOWN TO SEE HOW DEEP IT WAS.

WELL, DON'T JUST STAND THERE! EVERYBODY IS WAITING FOR YOU AT THE HOUSE!

GO IN! I'LL BE BACK SOON.

I'LL HAVE TO STEP CAREFULLY....

WHAT'S THAT?
TINK! CLINK!

OH, MY GOD! IT'S A GOAT!
CLINK! TINK!

HELP!
CLINK!

AAH!

OH, YOU STUPID BEAST!

I'M SORRY, SON. THIS GOAT IS SO WILD! IT MUST HAVE BROKEN THE ROPE.
AAH... ER... NEVER MIND!

COME IN! COME IN!

LATER, THE FAMILY SAT DOWN FOR A MEAL...

SUDDENLY—
OH! OH! THE GOAT AGAIN!
CLINK! TINK!

WHAM

AAH!
CLINK!
TINK!

YOU... I... ER...!
DON'T... AH...WORRY... OOH...!

MASTRAM HASTILY FINISHED HIS MEAL.
NO, THIS WON'T DO!

I HAVE GOT TO TELL SOME-ONE ABOUT MY PROBLEM.

LATER, WHEN HIS WIFE CAME IN—
WIFE, I HAVE TO TELL YOU SOMETHING.
YES?

I... ER... CAN SEE VERY WELL IN THE DAY TIME, BUT...
...NOT IN THE DARK, ISN'T THAT SO?

YES. AND THAT'S WHY I FELL IN THE GRAIN-PIT AND...
...STRUCK MOTHER.

I'M SORRY I DIDN'T TELL YOU EARLIER. BUT PLEASE HELP ME NOW. I MIGHT WANT TO GO OUT AT NIGHT.

THERE'S NO NEED TO WORRY. I'LL TIE A ROPE FROM THE BED TO THE YARD.

AND SO LATER THAT NIGHT WHEN MASTRAM HAD TO GO OUT TO ANSWER THE CALL OF NATURE —

I MUST SAY MY WIFE'S IDEA WAS A GOOD ONE.

NATURALLY HE DIDN'T SEE THE GOAT.

THE GOAT CHEWED THROUGH THE ROPE...
CHOMP! CHOMP!

...AND WHEN MASTRAM TURNED TO GO BACK—
THE ROPE IS GONE!

NOW IT'LL BE TOUGH GETTING BACK...

I'VE DONE IT!

HERE'S MY BED.

EEEIIIEEEEE

THIEF!! THIEF!!
GOOD HEAVENS! MOTHER-IN-LAW AGAIN! I'M IN THE WRONG ROOM!

MOTHER-IN-LAW, PLEASE DON'T PANIC. I AM MASTRAM.
YOU!

WHAT ARE YOU DOING HERE?
I CAME... I CAME...

...TO BEG YOUR PARDON FOR MY RUDE BEHAVIOUR THIS EVENING.

WHAT HAPPENED?
NOTHING! NOTHING!

WHAT A POLITE BOY YOU ARE! NOW GO AND SLEEP.

HEAVING A SIGH OF RELIEF, MASTRAM RETURNED TO HIS ROOM.
OOPS... WHAT A NARROW ESCAPE! BUT TOMORROW I MUST GO.
GO? GO WHERE?

TO THE CITY. TO GET THIS WRETCHED DISABILITY TREATED.

OUR SOLAR SYSTEM—1

Script: J.D. Isloor
Illustrations: Anand Mande

THERE ARE MANY MANY GALAXIES IN THE UNIVERSE.
ONE OF THEM WE CALL THE MILKY WAY.
THE MILKY WAY IS MADE UP OF COUNTLESS OF STARS.
AT ITS CENTRE, THE STARS ARE PACKED CLOSELY TOGETHER.
BUT THE STARS BECOME FEWER TOWARDS THE EDGE. TWO-THIRDS AWAY FROM THE CENTRE THERE IS AN ORDINARY, YELLOWISH STAR. THIS STAR IS OUR SUN AROUND WHICH OUR EARTH AND THE OTHER PLANETS REVOLVE.

FIVE PLANETS CAN BE SEEN WITH THE NAKED EYE.
SO IN ANCIENT TIMES AND EVEN AS LATE AS THE 18TH CENTURY PEOPLE THOUGHT THERE WERE ONLY FIVE OTHER PLANETS BESIDES EARTH.

EVERYONE WAS, THEREFORE, VERY SURPRISED WHEN AN ASTRONOMER NAMED HERSCHEL DISCOVERED A SEVENTH PLANET, URANUS, IN 1781.

URANUS AS IT MIGHT APPEAR FROM ITS SATELITE TITANIA

HERSCHEL DISCOVERED URANUS WITH A HUGE TELESCOPE HE HAD CONSTRUCTED.

YET ANOTHER PLANET WAS DISCOVERED IN 1846. IT WAS NAMED NEPTUNE.

NEPTUNE AND ITS TWO MOONS

IN 1930 A YOUNG ASTRONOMER NAMED CLYDE TOMBAUGH, DISCOVERED A NINTH PLANET. IT WAS NAMED PLUTO. CLYDE TOMBAUGH FOUND PLUTO BY STUDYING THOUSANDS OF PHOTOGRAPHS OF THE REGION OF THE SKY IN WHICH OTHER ASTRONOMERS HAD PREDICTED THAT PLUTO WOULD BE FOUND.

THE PLANETS

NAME IN ENGLISH	INDIAN NAME	YEAR OF DISCOVERY —
MERCURY	BUDHA	ANCIENT
VENUS	SHUKRA	ANCIENT
EARTH	BHUMANDAL PRITHVI	ANCIENT
MARS	MANGALA	ANCIENT
JUPITER	GURU BRIHASPATI	ANCIENT
SATURN	SHANI	ANCIENT
URANUS		1781
NEPTUNE		1846
PLUTO		1930

THE LOCKED POSTBOX

Readers' Choice

Illustrations : Jayanti Manoharan

Based on a story sent by Bhagat Chandra, Vasco-da-Gama

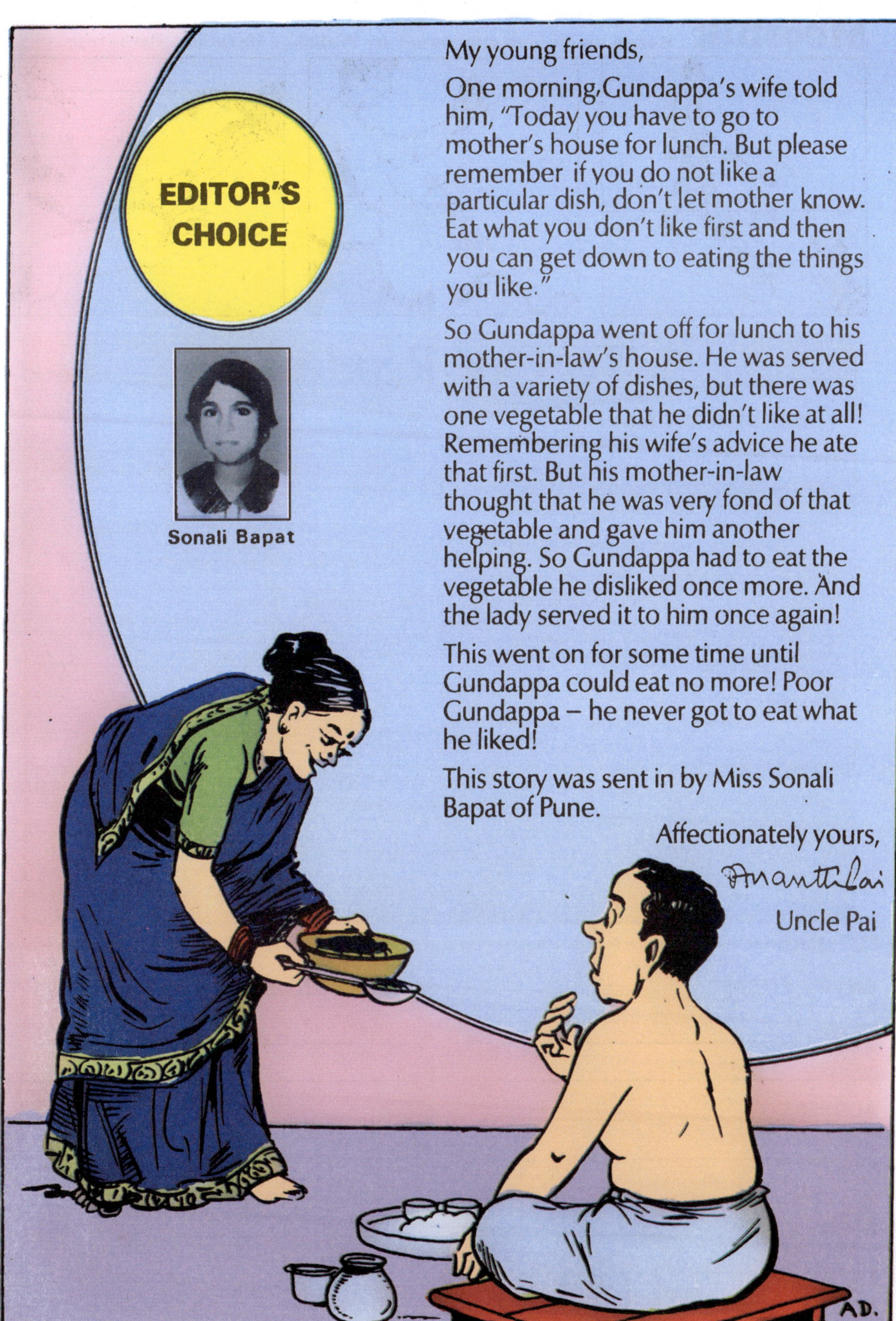

My young friends,

One morning, Gundappa's wife told him, "Today you have to go to mother's house for lunch. But please remember if you do not like a particular dish, don't let mother know. Eat what you don't like first and then you can get down to eating the things you like."

So Gundappa went off for lunch to his mother-in-law's house. He was served with a variety of dishes, but there was one vegetable that he didn't like at all! Remembering his wife's advice he ate that first. But his mother-in-law thought that he was very fond of that vegetable and gave him another helping. So Gundappa had to eat the vegetable he disliked once more. And the lady served it to him once again!

This went on for some time until Gundappa could eat no more! Poor Gundappa – he never got to eat what he liked!

This story was sent in by Miss Sonali Bapat of Pune.

Affectionately yours,

Ananth Pai

Uncle Pai

Mooshik

Based on an idea suggested by Prabahan Hazarika, Parbatpur

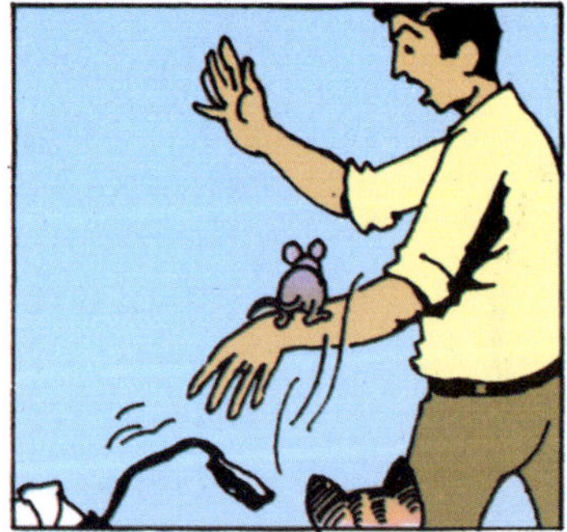

To Our Readers

TINKLE SUBSCRIPTIONS :
All new subscriptions and renewals of the old ones are accepted at :

PARTHA BOOKS DIVISION
Nav Prabhat Chambers, Ranade Road, Dadar, Bombay 400 028.
The annual subscription rate for 24 issues is Rs. 72/- per year (add Rs. 5/- on outstation cheques). Drafts/cheques/M.O. should be in favour of PARTHA BOOKS DIVISION.

Readers' Contributions should be addressed to Editor, TINKLE, Mahalaxmi Chambers (Basement), 22 Bhulabhai Desai Road, Bombay 400 026.

Mooshik :
Rs. 10/- will pe paid for every original idea accepted.

Readers' Choice :
* Please send only folktales you have heard and not those you have read in books, magazines or textbooks. Rs. 25/- will be paid for every accepted contribution.
* Send a self-addressed stamped envelope if you want the story to be returned.
* Please do not send photographs until asked for.

This happened to me :
You can write on your own strange, thrilling or amusing experience or adventure. Rs. 15/- will be paid for every accepted contribution

Readers Write...
1. Mail your letters to: Tinkle, P. Bag No. 16541, Bombay 400 026.
2. Please give your address in your letters, if you want a reply.

TINKLE TRICKS AND TREATS

1. Mail your entry to : Tinkle Competition Section, P. Bag No. 16541, Bombay 400 026
2. The first 50 all-correct entries received by us will each win a set of personal letterheads, with the winners'names and addresses printed on them !
3. The next 350 all-correct entries received by us will each win a copy of the AMAR INDIA WALL PAPER No. 23

CUT HERE

ENTRY FORM*

NAME : ____________________

____

ADDRESS : ____________________

____

____

STATE : ____________________

____

PIN ☐☐☐☐☐☐

MY SOLUTIONS TTT- 39

A ____________________

B ____________________

C _

—	—	—
|	—	—
|	|	—

* Refer to the footnote under the Editor's Note

Readers Write...

TINKLE No.44 helped me to do a project on satellites. You have been writing about some strange animals recently – the portuguese-man-of-war, the jacana and the platypus. Why don't you write on a common animal like the rabbit for a change?

Rajesh Parekh, Bangalore

Through TINKLE I would like to communicate with my friend Himanshu, who should now be in Calcutta. We have been out of touch for two years. So please include my letter to him.

Dear Himanshu,

It is over two years since we were last in contact with each other. I am now living in Bangalore. I hope that you will read this letter in TINKLE and write to me immediately.

Yours lovingly,
Ramakrishna Prasad
J-179, H.M.T., Bangalore 560 031

**(We sincerely hope that Himanshu will read this letter and write to Ramakrishna soon.
– Editor)**

I have a penfriend in London. We sometimes exchange gifts. For her birthday this year I sent her a bunch of TINKLE issues. After a while she wrote and thanked me for the wonderful gift. She said she liked TINKLE very much and has asked me to continue sending her copies!

Christie-Ann D'souza, Bombay

From the 42nd issue of TINKLE, it has become my favourite magazine. Can you guess why? Because in the Readers Write section you've printed Soumya Ghosh's letter – a letter of criticism. I have never before seen another comic magazine which has printed a critical letter.

Suhail Sheikh, Dharwar

I am a regular reader of TINKLE. My younger brother, Faisal, is usually very lazy in the mornings, but when a TINKLE issue arrives, he jumps out of bed and grabs it from me. He also is the first to get ready for school on that day! So for my brother's sake, please make TINKLE a weekly!

Farha Fatima, Hyderabad

Mooshik

Based on an idea suggested by Ajay Sharma, Calcutta

TINKLE TRICKS & TREATS*

TTT - 39

A Rearrange the pictures correctly to show the various stages of growth.

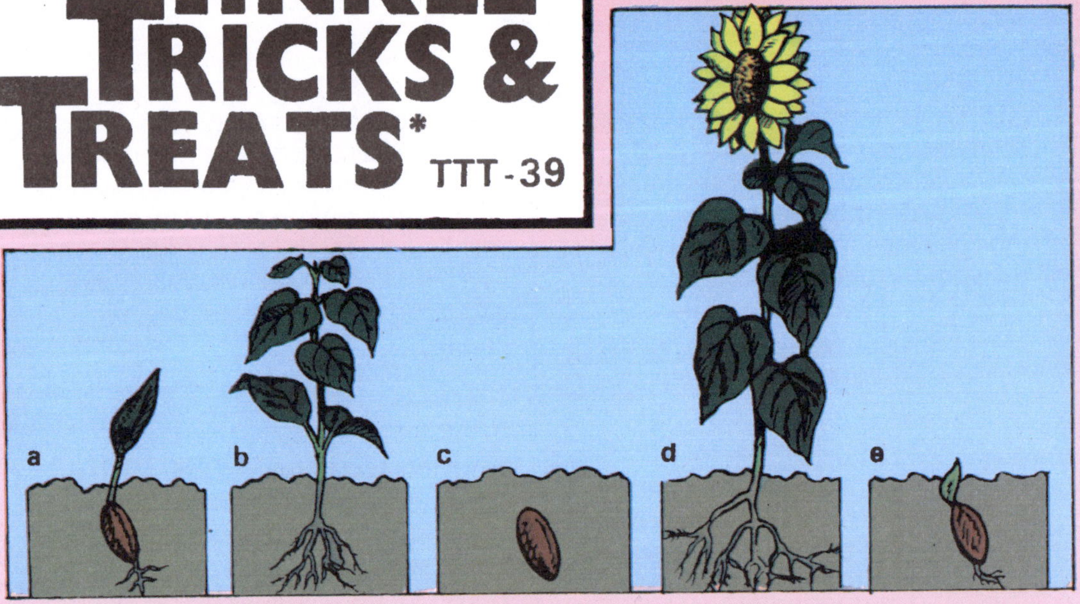

a b c d e

B How many of the numbers between 100 and 300 begin or end with 2?

C Complete the series.

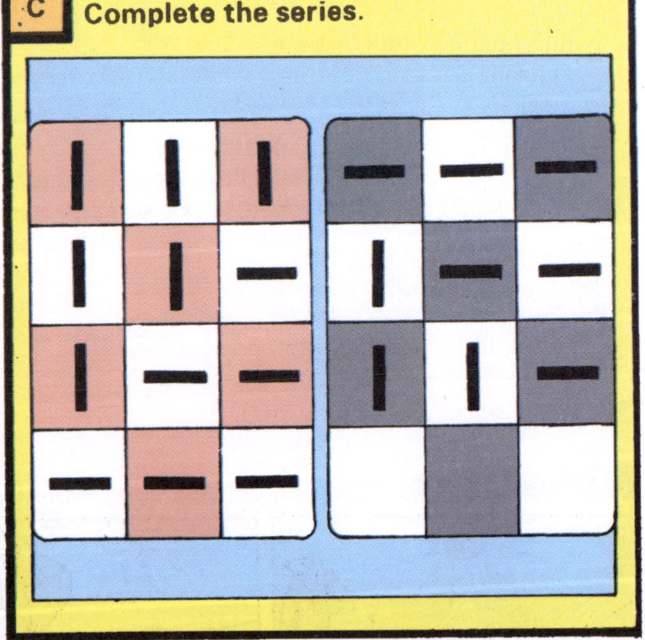

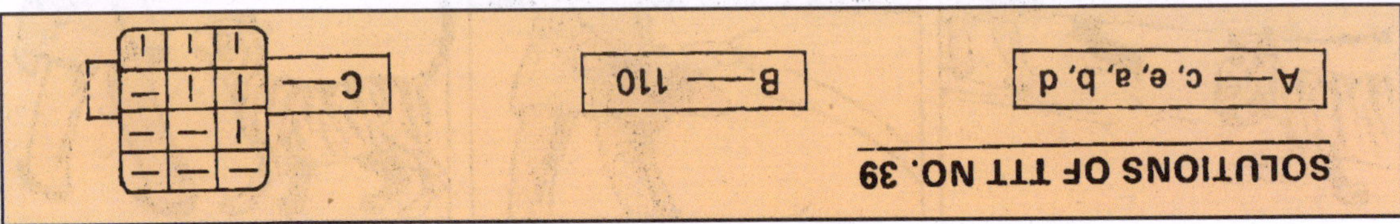

* Refer to the footnote under the Editor's Note

NO. 51
TINKLE
AMAR CHITRA KATHA
THE FORTNIGHTLY FOR CHILDREN FROM THE HOUSE OF AMAR CHITRA KATHA
TANTRI THE MANTRI
HOW THE GIRAFFE GOT HIS LONG NECK
THE LOTUS
Our National Flower

ABOUT

LETTERS FROM UNCLE PAI

Today the word *Tinkle* evokes many a reaction from older readers. Some respond with childish glee or start reminiscing about the tales of Kalia the Crow and their other favourite *Tinkle* Toons. Each reaction is always followed by a proud exclamation that they received a handwritten letter from Uncle Pai.

Letters from Uncle Pai to *Tinkle* readers across the country are the stuff of legend. Some have these letters framed in their houses. Some view the letters (whether positive or negative) as catalysts that pushed them back to the drawing board and on to the next story. Right from *Tinkle*'s very first issue, the office was flooded with story suggestions and feedback about the magazine. As the magazine grew and Storytime with Uncle Pai surged in popularity, the letters only kept increasing in number.

Mr. Pai made it a point to reply to every letter. Even when he had to write to a reader, rejecting their idea or story, they weren't your regular rejection letters. While a child was informed that their story wasn't chosen for publication, they were also encouraged to keep trying. Mr. Pai would often use examples of famous people who had failed before they finally succeeded. He urged readers never to give up and promised that their efforts would be rewarded.

It's no wonder then that these letters are cherished by older readers. Not only did they receive a signed letter from none other than Uncle Pai himself, but they also received a very valuable life lesson with it.

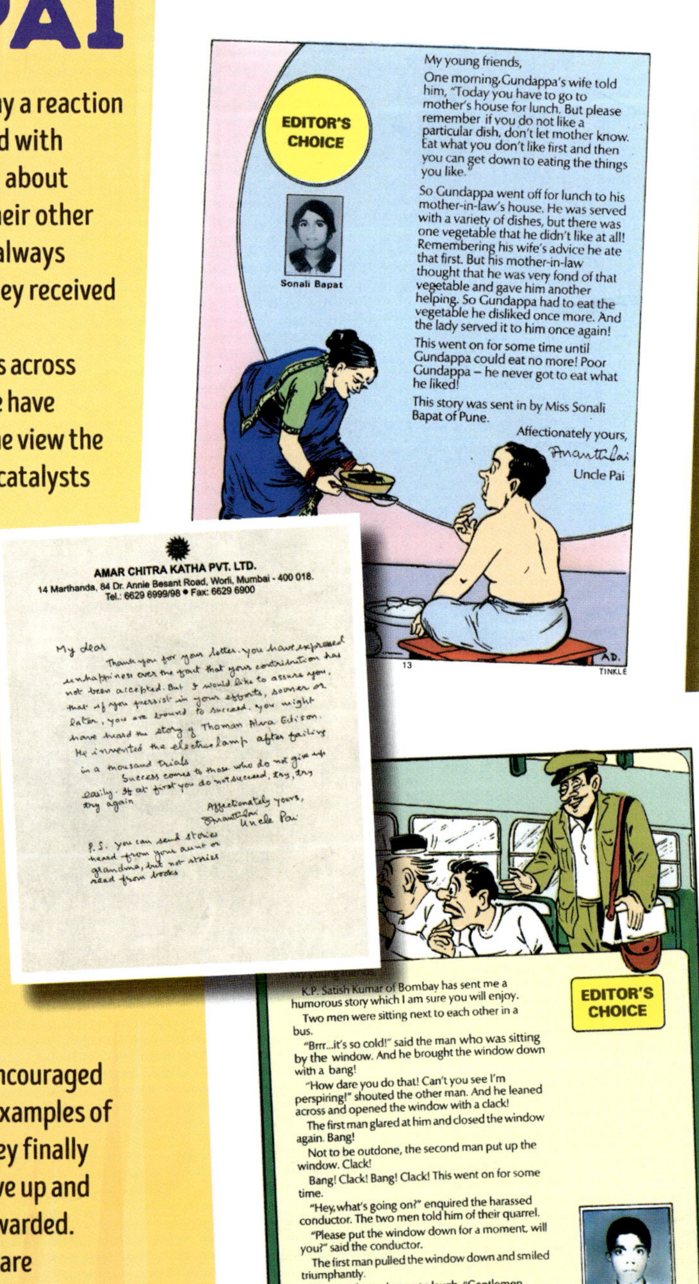

EDITOR'S CHOICE

Sonali Bapat

My young friends,

One morning, Gundappa's wife told him, "Today you have to go to mother's house for lunch. But please remember if you do not like a particular dish, don't let mother know. Eat what you don't like first and then you can get down to eating the things you like."

So Gundappa went off for lunch to his mother-in-law's house. He was served with a variety of dishes, but there was one vegetable that he didn't like at all! Remembering his wife's advice he ate that first. But his mother-in-law thought that he was very fond of that vegetable and gave him another helping. So Gundappa had to eat the vegetable he disliked once more. And the lady served it to him once again!

This went on for some time until Gundappa could eat no more! Poor Gundappa – he never got to eat what he liked!

This story was sent in by Miss Sonali Bapat of Pune.

Affectionately yours,

Ananth Pai

Uncle Pai

13 TINKLE

AMAR CHITRA KATHA PVT. LTD.
14 Marthanda, 84 Dr. Annie Besant Road, Worli, Mumbai - 400 018.
Tel.: 6629 6999/98 • Fax: 6629 6900

My dear

Thank you for your letter. You have expressed unhappiness over the fact that your contribution has not been accepted. But I would like to assure you, that if you persist in your efforts, sooner or later, you are bound to succeed. You might have heard the story of Thomas Alva Edison. He invented the electric lamp after failing in a thousand trials.

Success comes to those who do not give up easily. If at first you do not succeed, try, try try again

Affectionately yours,
Ananth Pai
Uncle Pai

P.S. You can send stories heard from your aunt or grandma, but not stories read from books

My young friends,

K.P. Satish Kumar of Bombay has sent me a humorous story which I am sure you will enjoy.

Two men were sitting next to each other in a bus.

"Brrr...it's so cold!" said the man who was sitting by the window. And he brought the window down with a bang!

"How dare you do that! Can't you see I'm perspiring!" shouted the other man. And he leaned across and opened the window with a clack!

The first man glared at him and closed the window again. Bang!

Not to be outdone, the second man put up the window. Clack!

Bang! Clack! Bang! Clack! This went on for some time.

"Hey, what's going on?" enquired the harassed conductor. The two men told him of their quarrel.

"Please put the window down for a moment, will you?" said the conductor.

The first man pulled the window down and smiled triumphantly.

The conductor began to laugh. "Gentlemen, please look closely at the window!"

The two men looked and what do you think they saw? There was no pane in the window!!!

Affectionately yours,

Ananth Pai

Uncle Pai

EDITOR'S CHOICE

Satish Kumar

TINKLE

D

Let's Make a Rock Pet!

You will need:

1. A few rocks of various shapes
2. Some enamel paints and brushes
3. Turpentine to clean stains

Clean each rock carefully. Then taking the natural shape of the rock into consideration, paint on it the features and limbs of some appropriate animal. Work very carefully and slowly.

Don't leave unpainted gaps. Fill up such spaces with drawings of flowers or other designs.

Let the rock dry completely — for at least two days. You can use the rock pet to decorate your shelf or as a paperweight.

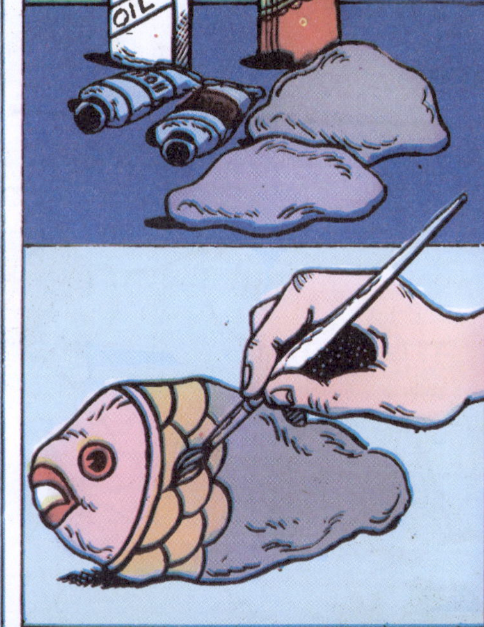

Readers' Choice

Outwitted by a Thief

Illustrations: Ashok Dongre

Story sent by N. Rajendran, Avanashi

GAWK

?
!

GROOP... AH... OOOH.

UNABLE TO SHOUT WITH THE FLOUR IN THEIR MOUTHS, THE TWO FOOLISH GIRLS WATCHED HELPLESSLY AS THE THIEF RAN AWAY WITH THEIR VALUABLES.

THE DODO

Script: Ashvin
Illustrations: Ajit Vasaikar

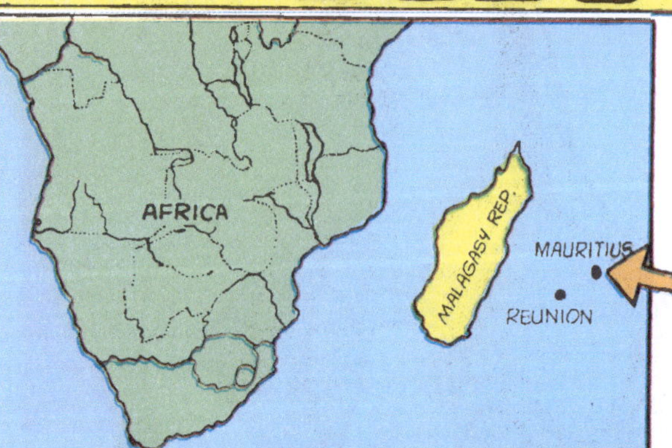

THE DODO WAS A LARGE BIRD WHICH ONCE LIVED ON THE ISLAND OF MAURITIUS.

IT COULDN'T FLY. IT WADDLED AROUND ON SHORT, STOUT LEGS.

THE SEED COULD NOT GET DIGESTED IN THE DODO'S STOMACH EITHER. AND IT WOULD BE THROWN OUT AS WASTE.

BUT AFTER PASSING THROUGH THE BIRD'S STOMACH, THE SHELL BECAME THINNER AND THEN THE SEED COULD START GROWING INTO A PLANT IF DROPPED IN THE SOIL.

SO THE DODO AND THE CALVARIA HELPED EACH OTHER. THE TREE PROVIDED THE BIRD WITH FRUITS AND THE DODO SOFTENED THE SEEDS OF THE TREE IN ITS STOMACH BEFORE DROPPING THEM IN THE SOIL.

IN 1507 EUROPEAN SAILORS LANDED ON MAURITIUS FOR THE FIRST TIME. AND FROM THEN ON MANY SHIPS BEGAN TO STOP AT THE ISLAND.

THE SAILORS WERE AMUSED BY THE LARGE AND CLUMSY DODOS AND THEY CHASED THE BIRDS AND KILLED THEM EITHER FOR FOOD OR JUST FOR FUN.

PIGS, BROUGHT BY THE SAILORS AND ALLOWED TO GO WILD, ATE THE BIRDS' EGGS.

SO MANY OF THESE GENTLE AND DEFENCELESS BIRDS WERE SLAUGHTERED THAT ONLY 85 YEARS AFTER MAN HAD FIRST SET FOOT ON MAURITIUS, THERE WERE NO DODOS LEFT ON THE ISLAND.

WHEN THE DODOS DISAPPEARED, THE CALVARIA MAJOR TREES LOST THEIR HELPERS.
NOW THERE WAS NO ONE TO PREPARE THE SEEDS FOR GROWTH.
NO MORE CALVARIA TREES HAVE GROWN SINCE THE DODOS DISAPPEARED.
THE TREES THAT REMAIN ARE VERY OLD AND DYING.

Complete-the-story competition No. 9*

THE BURGLAR

Illustrations: V. B. Halbe

What happens next?*

Complete this story in 200 words or less and send it to us by 28th February 1984 The best entry will win Rs. 50

* Refer to the footnote under the Editor's Note

THE KACHNAR

Script: J.D. Isloor
Illustrations: Anand Mande

THE SUN'S GIFTS*

Script: Nira Benegal
Illustrations: Dilip Kadam

* FROM THE MAHABHARATA

THIS JAMADAGNI IS GETTING RATHER TRYING.

I'LL STOP HIS WIFE FROM FETCHING MORE ARROWS.

IT'S BECOME HOTTER... I FEEL FAINT...

AAAAH!

RENUKA! WHERE ARE YOU? I NEED MORE ARROWS!

RENUKA!

IT'S TOO HOT TO RUN BACK AND FORTH...
WE MUSN'T GIVE UP, RENUKA! PLEASE BRING MORE ARROWS.

GOODNESS ME! I'LL HAVE TO DO SOMETHING TO MAKE THIS FOOLISH MAN STOP!

I'LL GO DOWN IN DISGUISE AND TALK TO HIM.

JAMADAGNI! WHAT ARE YOU DOING?

I'M TRYING TO GET EVEN WITH THE SUN FOR BEHAVING SO BADLY!

WHAT DID HE DO?
HE HAS MADE THE EARTH SO HOT! MY WIFE FAINTED JUST NOW!

I'LL BLAST HIM OUT OF THE SKY!
HE'S ONLY DOING HIS DUTY.

AND SO THE FIRST UMBRELLA AND THE FIRST PAIR OF CHAPPALS CAME INTO BEING.

Kalia
THE CROW
Illustrations :
RAM WAEERKAR

HOW MUCH FURTHER DO WE HAVE TO DRAG THIS LADDER?
NOT VERY FAR.

THERE'S THE TREE.

SHE HAS SEEN US.
NEVER MIND...

JUST KEEP GOING.
KEEP GOING?

BUT I THOUGHT IT WAS HER NEST WE WERE AFTER.
WE ARE... BUT KEEP GOING.

THIS IS FAR ENOUGH.
I COULDN'T... (GASP)... GO ANY FURTHER, ANYWAY.

BROTHER ELEPHANT, COULD YOU PROP THAT LADDER UP AGAINST THIS TREE?

NO NESTS IN THIS TREE.

NO HARM IN PROPPING THE LADDER UP, I SUPPOSE.

THERE YOU ARE!

STEADY, THERE! STEADY!

?

WHY IS HE CLIMBING THAT TREE?
KALIA!

HE'S...ER... GATHERING BERRIES.
HOW NICE.
BUT THERE ARE NO BERRIES ON THAT TREE!

I'VE A FEELING HE'S TRYING TO GET TO MOTHER HORNBILL'S NEST...

...ACROSS THE TREE TOPS. I'D BETTER GET HELP ... FAST!

THESE TREES ARE SO CLOSE TOGETHER, I CAN GO FROM ONE TO THE OTHER WITHOUT MUCH TROUBLE.

SOON I'LL BE AT THE NEST... HEEHEEHEE.
THERE HE IS BABLOO.

B-BABLOO.
CAN YOU SEE HIM?
YES!

GET DOWN, YOU HONEY-THIEF!

GET DOWN!
T-THERE'S NO HONEY HERE BABLOO.

I...OOPS.

THOD!

OOOOH!

K-KINDLY LET ME GO, SIR!

YAAAAAH!

KER-ASSSH!

HOURS LATER—
EXCUSE ME, WILL YOU HELP ME PROP UP THIS LADDER...
NO.

PATIENCE, CHAMATAKA, PATIENCE! SOMEONE IS BOUND TO HELP!

Readers' Choice

Again, Please!

Illustrations: Ram Waeerkar

Based on a story sent by Kamal Borah, Kohima

The Priest's Assistant

An Indian Folktale

Script : Gayatri M Dutt
Illustrations : Ashok Dongre

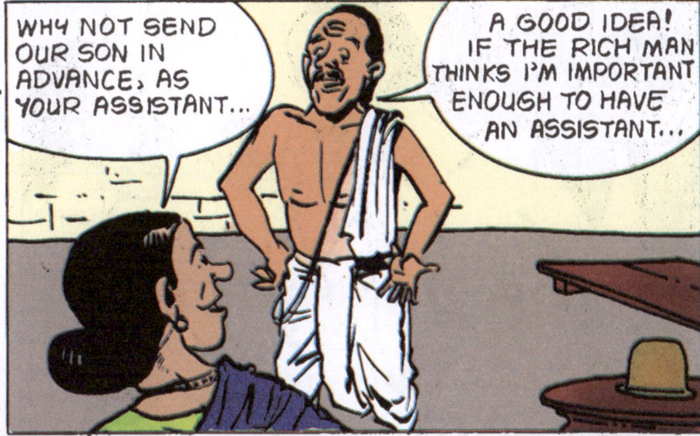

SO THE PRIEST EXPLAINED HIS PLAN TO HIS SON. THEN—
... BUT, MIND YOU, UNLIKE US THESE PEOPLE ARE RICH. THERE WILL BE CHAIRS AND TABLES AT THEIR HOUSE...

...SO BE SURE NOT TO SIT ON THE FLOOR. SIT ON A CHAIR, DO YOU HEAR ?

SIT ON A CHAIR... A HIGH SEAT... A SEAT THAT IS HIGHER THAN THE GROUND. DO YOU UNDERSTAND?
OH, YES, YES, CERTAINLY!

AND TALK SENSIBLY AND ON IMPORTANT MATTERS.
WHAT ?

HELP ME, GOD !

I SAID, TALK ON SERIOUS TOPICS... WEIGHTY MATTERS. DOES THAT MAKE SENSE TO YOU ?
WEIGHTY MATTERS? FINE, FINE! DON'T WORRY.

SO WITH HIS FATHER'S ADVICE IN MIND, THE YOUTH SET OFF AND SOON ARRIVED AT THE RICH MAN'S HOUSE.
HE MUST BE THE PRIEST'S ASSISTANT.

HE WAS GIVEN A WARM WELCOME —
COME, PLEASE TAKE A SEAT.

SHE'S OFFERING ME A MAT TO SIT ON. BUT FATHER SAID...

THE YOUNG PRIEST LOOKED THIS WAY AND THAT...

... AND THEN MADE STRAIGHT FOR THE COW-SHED IN THE COURTYARD.

DONE IT! AND NOW I MUST TALK ABOUT HEAVY THINGS!

ER... WHAT ARE YOU DOING UP THERE? PLEASE COME DOWN.

HAMMER-HEAD.
WHAT?

WHY MUST YOU SIT THERE? COME INTO THE HOUSE.

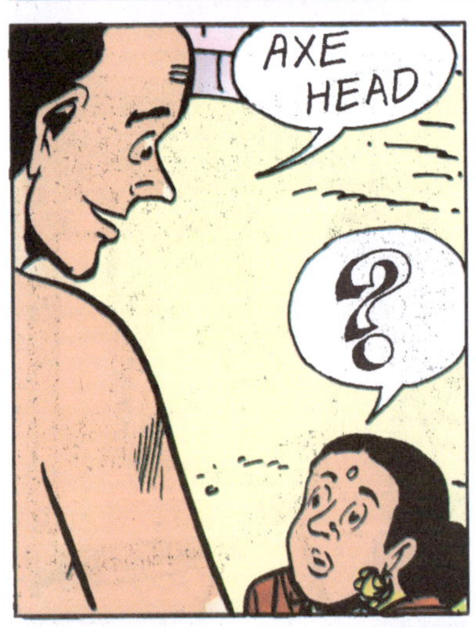
AXE HEAD
?

I DON'T UNDERSTAND. PLEASE COME INSIDE.
GRINDING STONE.

HE'S GONE MAD!!

JUST THEN, THE PRIEST ARRIVED. WHEN HE HEARD WHAT HAD HAPPENED, HE FLUSHED WITH EMBARRASSMENT.
ME AND MY GRAND IDEAS!

AND GOING INTO THE COW-SHED, HE STERNLY ORDERED HIS SON TO COME DOWN!

POLLINATION
Script: Prof. (Mrs.) S.M. Almeida
Illustrations: J.P. Irani
PUSH ASIDE THE PETALS OF A FLOWER AND YOU'LL SEE THE PISTIL, THE FEMALE PART OF THE FLOWER. THE BOTTOM OF THE PISTIL IS USUALLY THICKENED. THIS PART IS CALLED THE OVARY. THE OVARY CONTAINS THE OVULES.
STAMEN.
PISTIL
OVULES
OVARY
AROUND THE PISTIL STAND A CROWD OF STAMENS. THE STAMENS ARE THE MALE PARTS OF THE FLOWER. THEY PRODUCE A YELLOW DUST CALLED POLLEN.
MALE FLOWER
FEMALE FLOWER
SOMETIMES YOU'LL COME ACROSS FLOWERS HAVING ONLY STAMENS OR ONLY PISTILS. PAPAYA TREES FOR EXAMPLE, ARE EITHER WHOLLY MALE OR WHOLLY FEMALE. THE FLOWERS OF THE MALE PAPAYA TREE HAVE ONLY STAMENS. AND THE FLOWERS OF THE FEMALE PAPAYA TREE, ONLY PISTILS.
MALE FLOWER
FEMALE FLOWER
ALL GOURDS LIKE PUMPKINS, MELONS AND CUCUMBERS HAVE SEPARATE MALE AND FEMALE FLOWERS ON THE SAME VINE. THE MALE FLOWERS HAVE ONLY STAMENS. AND THE FEMALE FLOWERS HAVE ONLY PISTILS.
SOME PLANTS LIKE THE MANGO TREE AND THE CASHEW-NUT TREE HAVE SEPARATE MALE AND FEMALE FLOWERS GROWING ON THE SAME TREE – AND ALSO FLOWERS WHICH HAVE BOTH MALE AND FEMALE PARTS.
YOUNG CASHEW FRUIT.
MANGO FLOWER

THE TRANSFER OF POLLEN GRAINS FROM STAMENS TO PISTILS IS CALLED POLLINATION. SOMETIMES THE POLLEN IS CARRIED BY WIND...
HONEY BEE
BUMBLE BEE
WASP
BUTTER FLY
...SOMETIMES BY INSECTS AND BIRDS. FLOWERS PRODUCE NECTAR SO THAT INSECTS AND BIRDS WILL COME TO THEM.
WHEN AN INSECT IS FEEDING ON NECTAR, POLLEN FROM THE FLOWER GETS RUBBED OFF ON ITS BODY...
...AND WHEN IT FLIES TO ANOTHER FLOWER TO FEED ON MORE NECTAR, SOME OF THE POLLEN WHICH IS STICKING TO ITS BODY MIGHT GET RUBBED OFF ON THE PISTIL OF THAT FLOWER.
FLOWERS WHICH OPEN IN THE NIGHT ARE USUALLY SWEET-SCENTED. THEIR POLLEN IS CARRIED FROM ONE FLOWER TO ANOTHER BY MOTHS...
... OR BATS.
ENLARGED WASP
FIGS CONTAIN HUNDREDS OF VERY SMALL MALE AND FEMALE FLOWERS. THESE GET POLLINATED BY TINY WASPS AND ANTS.
MALE FLOWER
FEMALE FLOWER
IN THE CASE OF WATER PLANTS, IT IS THE WATER WHICH CARRIES POLLEN FROM FLOWER TO FLOWER.
FEMALE FLOWER
MALE FLOWER

THE SEVENTH IDLI
Script:
Rina Mukherji
Illustrations:
Sumitra S. Sawant

VISHNUDUTT WAS VERY HUNGRY.
AH, THERE'S A MAN SELLING IDLIS!

HOW MUCH FOR THE IDLIS?
EIGHT FOR A RUPEE.

HERE'S A RUPEE.
AND HERE ARE YOUR IDLIS.

THEY'RE SO FLUFFY AND DELICIOUS

HERE GOES THE SEVENTH ONE!

OH, NO!

WAAA!

WHAT'S THE MATTER, DEAR MAN ? DO TELL US.
WHAT A FOOL I HAVE BEEN!

I BOUGHT EIGHT IDLIS FOR A RUPEE AND ATE SIX OF THEM.

BUT IT WAS ONLY THE SEVENTH ONE WHICH SATISFIED MY HUNGER.
IF I HAD EATEN THE SEVENTH ONE FIRST I COULD HAVE SAVED THE OTHERS!

HAVE YOU EVER SEEN A BIGGER FOOL THAN ME?
NO, NEVER!

THE TOY MOUSE

READERS' CHOICE

Illustrations: Dilip Kadam

Based on a story sent by Robert Gonsalves, Bardez

NEWS OF THE UNUSUAL COMPETITION SPREAD.
A MOUSE? THAT SHOULD BE AN EASY THING TO MAKE.

EVERYWHERE PEOPLE BEGAN TO MAKE TOY MICE.

AND ON THE DAY OF THE CONTEST THEY ALL CAME TO THE MILLIONAIRE'S HOUSE—
MY MOUSE WILL SURELY BAG THE PRIZE.
NO, MINE WILL. IT'S BIGGER AND FATTER THAN YOURS.

BUT ONE MOUSE DID NOT LOOK LIKE A MOUSE AT ALL.
IS THAT MEANT TO BE A MOUSE?
YES, IT IS.

LISTEN, BOY! WHY DON'T YOU GO HOME? YOU DON'T STAND A CHANCE WITH THAT THING!
HAH! HAH! HAH!

HUSH! HERE COMES OUR PATRON!

YOU WILL ALL ARRANGE YOUR MICE ON THE PLATFORM AND THEN I WILL RELEASE MY CAT.

THE ONE SHE PICKS WILL WIN THE PRIZE.

SOON...
ONE... TWO...THREE.. GO GET IT!

THERE! SHE HAS POUNCED ON ONE RIGHT AWAY!
WHO'S THE WINNER?

THE BOY! I CAN'T BELIEVE IT!
IMPOSSIBLE!

I... I... PROTEST! THIS IS UNFAIR!
SO DO I... OUR MICE ARE SO MUCH BETTER THAN THAT THING. IT DOES NOT EVEN LOOK LIKE A MOUSE.

GENTLEMEN, YOU MUST ADMIT THAT THE CAT KNOWS BEST!

AFTER THE BOY HAD RECEIVED HIS PRIZE —
TELL ME, MY BOY. WHY DID THE CAT CHOOSE YOUR MOUSE?
PERHAPS IT WAS HUNGRY...

...I MADE MY MOUSE OUT OF SALTED FISH!

My young friends,

K.P. Satish Kumar of Bombay has sent me a humorous story which I am sure you will enjoy.

EDITOR'S CHOICE

Two men were sitting next to each other in a bus.

"Brrr...it's so cold!" said the man who was sitting by the window. And he brought the window down with a bang!

"How dare you do that! Can't you see I'm perspiring!" shouted the other man. And he leaned across and opened the window with a clack!

The first man glared at him and closed the window again. Bang!

Not to be outdone, the second man put up the window. Clack!

Bang! Clack! Bang! Clack! This went on for some time.

"Hey, what's going on?" enquired the harassed conductor. The two men told him of their quarrel.

"Please put the window down for a moment, will you?" said the conductor.

The first man pulled the window down and smiled triumphantly.

The conductor began to laugh. "Gentlemen, please look closely at the window!"

The two men looked and what do you think they saw? There was no pane in the window!!!

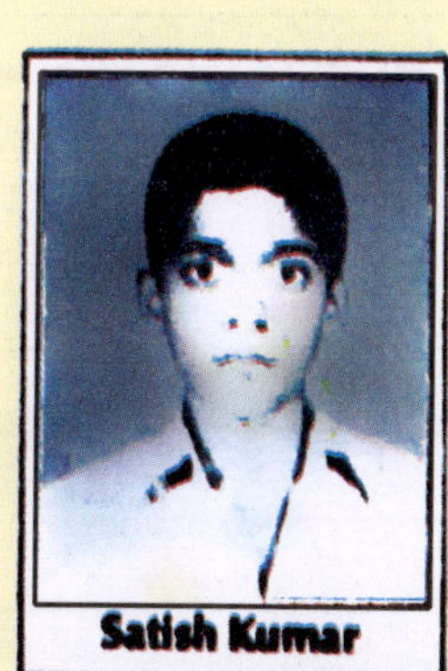

Satish Kumar

Affectionately yours,

Anant Pai

Uncle Pai

Mooshik Based on an idea suggested by Ravi S. Pednekar, Bhayandar

Readers Write...

I read the story about Nasruddin Hodja in TINKLE No: 42 and soon after I was asked by my teacher to tell a short story. Before I began, I asked the class, "Do any of you know what I'm going to tell you?" The whole class said, "No!" So I began to narrate the story of Hodja and soon my audience was rolling around, laughing!

Bendangmeren, Nagaland

I would like it if you could print adventurous, yet simple stories which children of 7 years will understand. (I'm seven!) Secretly, I also hope you will publish this letter in Readers Write!

Paromeeta Mathur, Calcutta

The hilarious adventures of Shikari Shambhu are very interesting and humorous. I'm sure all TINKLE readers must be appreciating this feature.

V. N. V. Bhaskar, Vijayawada

My grandfather spent a month with us recently. After a few days he began to feel bored, so I gave him my TINKLE copies to read. Suddenly he was bored no longer!

Cyriac Joseph, B.E.M.L. Nagar

My friends and I liked the story "The Adventure of Kasperle" so much that we staged this drama in our club. Everybody enjoyed it and it was a success.

Shiladitya Dasgupta, Jamnagar

CUT HERE

ENTRY FORM*

Say it Yourself – 8

NAME : ____________________

____

ADDRESS : ____________________

____

____

STATE : ____________________

PIN : ____________________

Answer: ____________________

* Refer to the footnote under the Editor's Note

ANWAR
by
Appaswami
Illustrations: V. B. Halbe

WE WOULD LIKE TO BUY A HELICOPTER...
... FOR OUR SON.

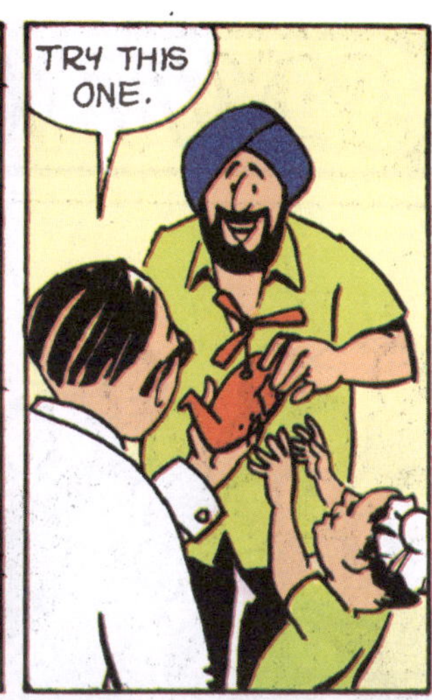
TRY THIS ONE.

PLEASE SHOW ME THAT PLANE...

ZOOM

HEY, INDER! WHAT ARE YOU DOING HERE?
I'M WAITING FOR DAD AND MUM.

THEY ARE BUSY PLAYING INSIDE.

SAY IT YOURSELF AND WIN A CASH PRIZE* NO. 8

A.D.

WENDY, IF YOU'RE SO FOND OF TALKING, WHY HAVEN'T YOU ENTERED THE ELOCUTION CONTEST?

WHAT DO YOU THINK IS WENDY'S REPLY?

1. Mail your entry to:
   TINKLE Competition Section,
   P. Bag No. 16541, Bombay 400026
2. • First prize : Rs. 50/- • Second prize : Rs. 25/- • Third prize : Rs. 15/- • 10 Consolation prizes : Rs. 10/- each
3. Decision of the judges is final and binding. Names of the prize-winners will be announced in TINKLE No. 57
4. Entry form for Say It Yourself No. 8 is given on page No. 14

Last date for receiving entries: 10.3.1984

* Refer to the footnote under the Editor's Note

Results of Say it Yourself No. 6*

FIRST PRIZE C.R. Sudhakar, 7-5-629/12, Bharathi Bldg. Sultan Battery Road, Mangalore

SECOND PRIZE Shashvat Dayal, Bombay

THIRD PRIZE Asha Bhaskaran, Bombay AND Ajay Singh, New Delhi

Consolation Prizes of Rs. 10 each

Aparna Jetly
New Delhi

Deepak Mirchandani
Bombay

Aftab Latheef
Pune

Smita Gupta
Bombay

Anupam Taneja
Chandigarh

Veena S. Ahuja
Bombay

Ranjan Ramnath
Bangalore

Nakul Pasricha
New Delhi

D. Umashankar
Bangalore

Hiral S. Chandarana
Mangalore

THE BUS DRIVER'S REPLY:

Sorry, I could wash only one side !

Prize-winning entry from C.R. Sudhakar

NO. 52

Rs. 3

TINKLE

AMAR CHITRA KATHA

THE FORTNIGHTLY FOR CHILDREN FROM THE HOUSE OF AMAR CHITRA KATHA

THE DODO

OUR SOLAR SYSTEM

THE ADVENTURES OF A SON-IN-LAW

CHANDRAKANT RANE

Mr. Chandrakant Rane was a lettering artist who worked with *Rang Rekha Features**. In 1975, Mr. Anant Pai asked him to join *Amar Chitra Katha (ACK)*.

Mr. Rane joined the *Tinkle* Team in June 1981. Initially, he worked as a freelancer and stuck to lettering. But eventually, he began illustrating and colouring for *ACK*.

At the time, all the processes involved in comic making were manual, i.e. done by hand, including the lettering. Mr. Rane was a very talented letterer and chose crowquill nib pens while his peers had moved on to rotring (mechanical) pens**, which were more convenient.

Mr. Rane had an eye for composition and was responsible for the art of the *Tinkle Digest* covers in its early years. He didn't just pick and paste images from different stories together. He individually traced the art from the stories he liked, and drew and coloured them especially for the cover.

He preferred to illustrate in the realistic style. His work reflected his patience, dedication and skill.

Mr. Rane was the Art Director for *Tinkle* when the comic-making process switched to computers around 1998-99. He was the first from the team to learn such new software as Adobe Photoshop and Illustrator. As for the team he led, he encouraged them to learn these software and got them enrolled in courses to update their knowledge.

Mr. Rane was always patient and considerate in his relations with his colleagues. He encouraged the artists he worked with to develop their own style. Regarded as a fine professional guide, he had a good rapport with staff and freelancers alike.

** India's first comic and cartoon syndicate founded by Anant Pai. It supplied comic strip content to a number of newspapers.*
***Crowquill pens had detachable nibs which would have to be dipped in ink to use, while rotring pens could be filled with ink like fountain pens. Thus, rotring pens were easier to use.*

DID YOU KNOW?

Badminton originated in India several hundred years ago. The game was introduced into England in 1873 and became popular at Badminton in Gloucestershire, from where it acquired its name.

Badminton can be played indoors or outdoors. It is played with a light stringed racket and a shuttlecock. The shuttlecock is made of goose feathers in a cork or plastic base.

The shuttlecock is served and play continues so long as the shuttlecock does not touch the ground or go out of the court. Three games make a set and a game is won by the first side to make 15 points. Only the side which is serving can score.

Badminton is a very fast game and excellent exercise. It can be played by two persons (singles) or by four (doubles).

One of the greatest badminton players in the world is Prakash Padukone of India.

THE MERCHANT AND THE PARROT

Illustrations: Souren Roy

Readers' Choice

Based on a story sent by Suchandra Bhattacharya, Shillong

O GREEN-FEATHERED FRIENDS! I WANT TO KNOW SOMETHING FROM YOU.

MY HIRAMAN, WHO LIVES IN A CAGE, WANTS TO KNOW HOW TO ESCAPE.

HEARING THIS A PARROT FELL DEAD.

WHEN THE MERCHANT RETURNED HOME—
DID YOU ASK THE PARROTS?
YES.

BUT WHEN I DID SO, ONE OF THEM FELL DEAD ON THE SPOT.

OH!

POOR HIRAMAN! I KNEW HE WAS TOO SOFT-HEARTED TO HEAR SUCH SAD NEWS.

?

THAT PARROT IN BENGAL DID NOT REALLY DIE, YOU KNOW...

HE MERELY ACTED OUT THE TRICK I SHOULD PLAY ON YOU.
YOU PARROTS ARE INDEED VERY CLEVER.

WELL, GOODBYE MY FRIEND.

Joseph Lister

Based on material provided by Dr. S.G. Kabra

Illustrations : Anand Mande

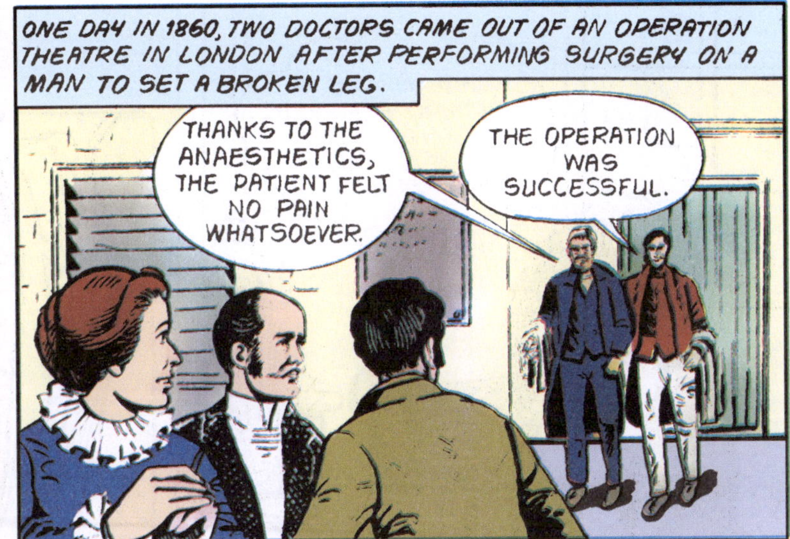

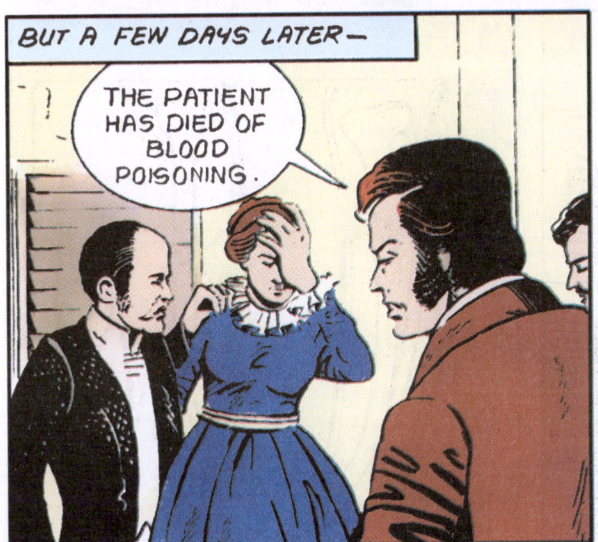

IN A SIMPLE FRACTURE THE BROKEN BONES DO NOT COME OUT OF THE SKIN.

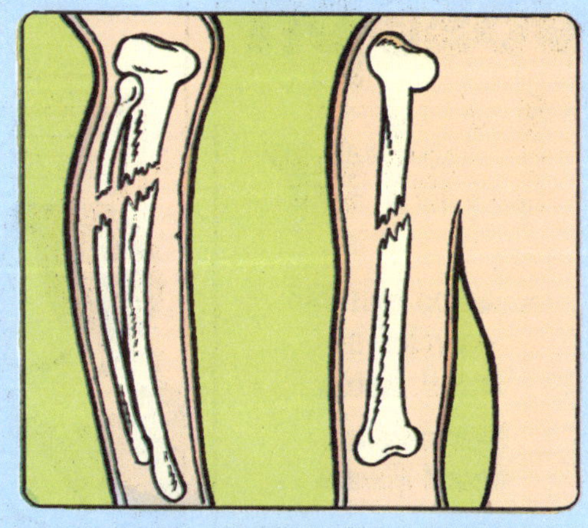

IN A COMPOUND FRACTURE THE BONES BREAK THROUGH THE SKIN AND THE WOUND IS EXPOSED TO THE AIR.

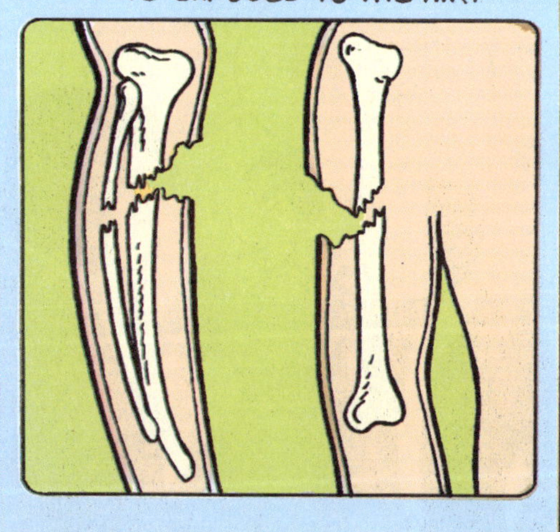

THEN ONE DAY HE READ A REPORT BY THE FRENCH SCIENTIST, LOUIS PASTEUR. LOUIS PASTEUR HAD FOUND OUT THAT THERE WERE TINY LIVING CREATURES (GERMS) IN THE AIR WHICH CAUSED THINGS TO GO BAD.

SO IT'S NOT THE AIR ITSELF WHICH CAUSES THINGS TO GO BAD. IT IS THE GERMS IN THE AIR.

ON AUGUST 2, 1865, A BOY WITH COMPOUND FRACTURE OF LEG BONES WAS BROUGHT TO HIM. LISTER SET THE BONES AND HAD CARBOLIC ACID APPLIED TO THE AREA OF THE WOUND. HE THEN COVERED IT WITH TIN FOIL AND A BANDAGE.

LISTER SPENT THREE RESTLESS DAYS HOPING FOR THE SUCCESS OF THIS METHOD OF TREATMENT.

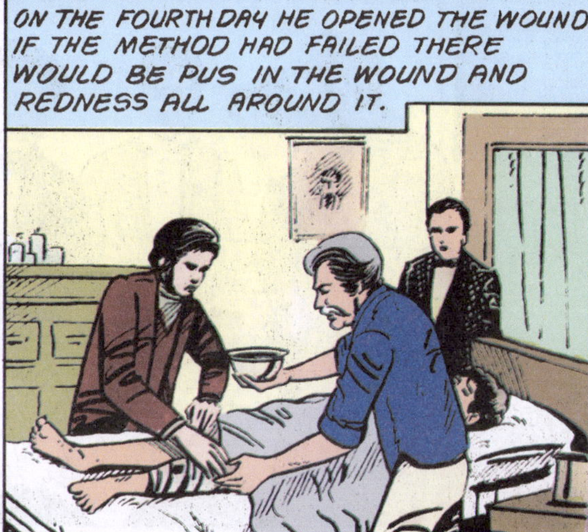
ON THE FOURTH DAY HE OPENED THE WOUND. IF THE METHOD HAD FAILED THERE WOULD BE PUS IN THE WOUND AND REDNESS ALL AROUND IT.

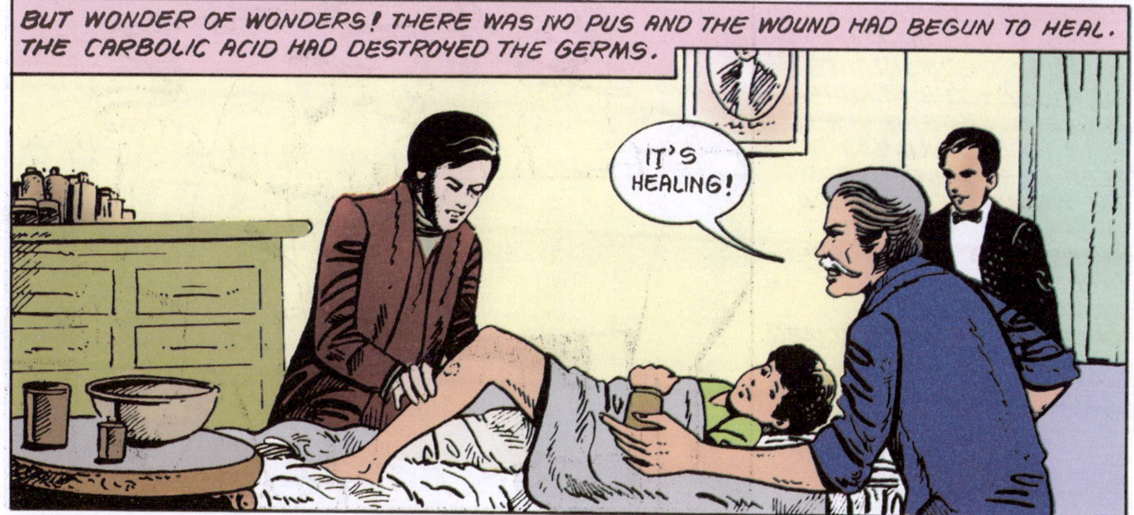
BUT WONDER OF WONDERS! THERE WAS NO PUS AND THE WOUND HAD BEGUN TO HEAL. THE CARBOLIC ACID HAD DESTROYED THE GERMS.
IT'S HEALING!

LISTER NOW BEGAN DRESSING ALL WOUNDS WITH A SOLUTION OF CARBOLIC ACID. DURING OPERATIONS, HE HAD A MAN SPRAY THIS SOLUTION, OVER THE OPERATING TABLE WITH A SPRAY PUMP. AFTER THE OPERATION, HE DRESSED THE CUT WITH CARBOLIC ACID HE ALSO BEGAN TO WASH HIS HANDS CAREFULLY BEFORE ANY OPERATION. AND HE KEPT THE OPERATING INSTRUMENTS IN CARBOLIC ACID.

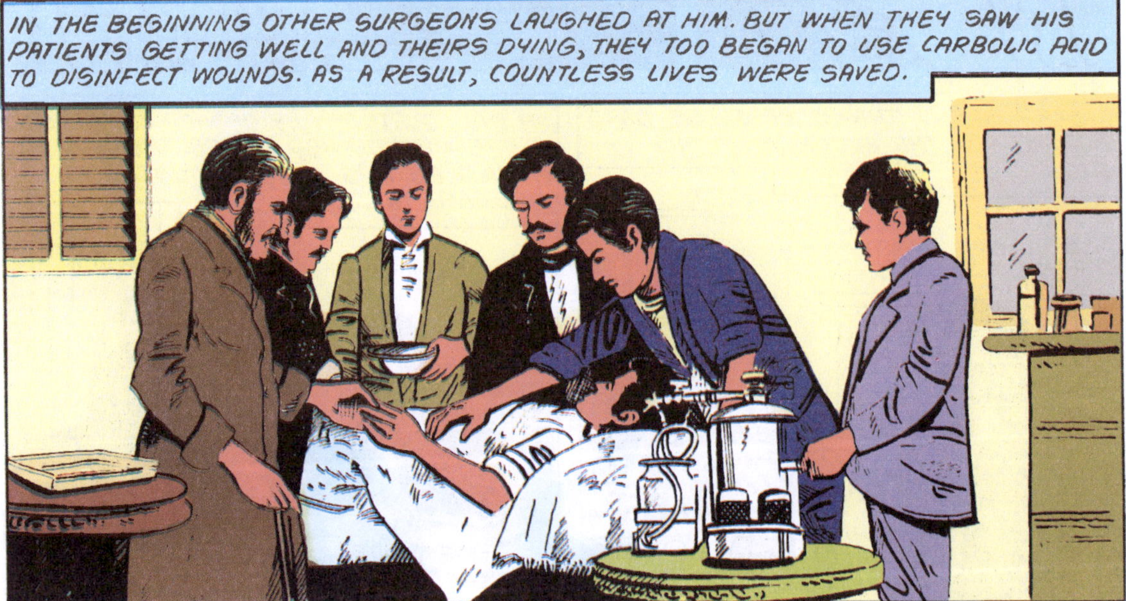

SURGEONS TODAY NO LONGER USE DISINFECTANTS LIKE CARBOLIC ACID ON WOUNDS BECAUSE DISINFECTANTS SLOW DOWN THE HEALING PROCESS. INSTEAD THEY RELY ON CLEANLINESS TO KEEP GERMS AWAY FROM THE WOUND. IN A MODERN OPERATING ROOM, EVERYTHING IS SPOTLESSLY CLEAN AND ALL INSTRUMENTS AND DRESSINGS ARE STERILIZED.

A MATTER OF PAYMENT

Based on a story sent by Dilip Kesari, Jharia

Illustrations: Ram Waeerkar

AH! THAT WAS GOOD!

WHAT'S THIS? A BILL FOR EIGHTY RUPEES!

YOU HAVE WRITTEN OUTSIDE THAT BILLS WILL BE RECOVERED FROM ONE'S HEIRS!!!
YOU ARE RIGHT, SIR. THIS IS NOT YOUR BILL...

...IT'S YOUR FATHER'S!

R.W.

TANTRI THE MANTRI

Script : Appaswami
Illustrations: Ashok Dongre

YOU CAN COME DOWN NOW, SIR.

LATER—
HE'S A ROGUE!...
... AND ALWAYS RUNNING AWAY.

IN SHORT, A DANGEROUS ANIMAL, EH?

BRING HIM TO THE PALACE.

I'LL SEND RAJA HOOJA ON AN ELEPHANT RIDE.

AND SOON, I'LL BE THE RAJA, NOT HOOJA.

HERE WE ARE.
WHERE IS THE MANTRI?

MAHARAJ! THIS IS THE ELEPHANT I WANT YOU TO RIDE.
ALL RIGHT.

HERE WE GO.

LET GO THE ROPES, YOU FOOLS!

THUD! THUD!

NOW I WILL BE THE RAJA, INSTEAD OF HOOJA!
CRACK

THUDDD
OUCH!!

HELP!

GET THIS TREE OFF ME!

OUCH!

LATER—
TANTRI! THE TREE FELL, REVEALING A BURIED TREASURE!

BUT TELL ME, IS THERE NO SIMPLER WAY OF FINDING BURIED TREASURE?

RAMESH EARNS A PILE

Illustrations : Ram Waeerkar

Readers' Choice

Based on a story sent by K. Srinivasan, Coimbatore

HURRICANE THAT HID IN A TREE
Script: Rina Mukherjee
Illustrations: V.B. Halbe
ON THE OUTSKIRTS OF A JUNGLE, LIVED AN OLD WOMAN WITH HER GRANDSON, CHANDU.

CHANDU TOOK HIS SHEEP TO GRAZE IN THE JUNGLE. ONE DAY—
SHEEP!

I'LL GRAB ONE WHEN THE BOY IS NOT LOOKING.

SUDDENLY—
CHANDU! OH, CHANDU!

COME HOME QUICKLY! THERE'S A HURRICANE COMING THIS WAY!

A HURRICANE!

BOTH THE OLD LADY AND THE BOY SEEM TO BE TERRIFIED. HURRICANE MUST BE A DEMON!

W-WHAT IF IT CATCHES ME!

AEEII... I'D BETTER HIDE SOMEWHERE.

I KNOW! I'LL MINGLE WITH THE SHEEP AND HIDE IN THE SHEEPFOLD.

HURRY! HURRY!

GET IN, ALL OF YOU.

THE LEOPARD ENTERED THE BARN...

... AND WAS SHUT IN.
I'M SAFE HERE.

BUT JUST BEFORE DAWN—
CREAK!

SOMEBODY'S COMING IN!

IT MUST BE HURRICANE!

I- IT'S TOUCHING ME!

NOW IT'S PUTTING A SACK OVER ME.

BUT I'D BETTER NOT MAKE A SOUND.

I HOPE YOU GOT A BIG SHEEP.
THE BIGGEST! HELP ME DRAG IT AWAY.

THIS MUST BE THE HEAVIEST SHEEP WE'VE EVER STOLEN.

THE SUN'S COMING UP! LET'S OPEN THE SACK AND MAKE THE ANIMAL WALK.

WHEN THE SACK WAS OPENED—
?!

IT-IT'S A LEOPARD!

RUN!

HURRICANE HAS GONE INTO THAT HOLLOW.

NOW'S MY CHANCE TO ESCAPE.

?!

WHAT'S THE MATTER, BROTHER?

I'M FLEEING FROM HURRICANE!

HURRICANE! AND WHAT'S THAT?
A TERRIBLE CREATURE. IT DRAGGED ME OVER HALF THE JUNGLE.

IT SEEMS TO ME THAT YOU'RE EASILY FRIGHTENED!

COME, SHOW ME WHERE THIS HURRICANE LIVES.

CAN YOU SEE THAT TREE? IT'S INSIDE THAT.
SO IT HIDES IN TREES!

I'LL CLIMB UP AND FEEL THE CREATURE WITH MY TAIL.

A B-BEAR'S CLIMBING UP!

WHAT'S IT DOING?
GRAB ITS TAIL!

IT HAS CAUGHT MY TAIL! AAAH!

THE TERRIFIED BEAR PULLED FREE...

...LOST ITS BALANCE AND FELL—

THUD

IT'S TRULY A MONSTER!

YOU WERE RIGHT, BROTHER. IT IS AN AWFUL CREATURE.
DIDN'T I TELL YOU?

ER... IT MAY BE FOLLOWING ME!
LET'S RUN!

?

WAIT!

WHO'S CHASING YOU?
WE ARE FLEEING FROM HURRICANE.

HURRICANE! AND WHAT IS THAT?
OH, IT IS SIMPLY AWFUL! A CREATURE THAT DRAGS AND PULLS ANIMALS.

I MARVEL AT YOUR COWARDICE. WE JUNGLE FOLK SHOULD NEVER BE FRIGHTENED OF ANYONE.

COME, SHOW ME THE CREATURE!

LOOK, THERE IS THE TREE. HURRICANE STAYS WITHIN IT. BE CAREFUL THOUGH.
YOU NEEDN'T WORRY!

IT'S A TIGER THIS TIME! GOD HAVE MERCY ON US!

I'LL STEP OUT AND SEE WHAT IT IS DOING.

OOPS!

AAAAH!

THUMP!

HURRICANE HAS JUMPED ON MY BACK!

AIEE!!

THE SOONER I REACH MY FRIENDS, THE BETTER... AH, THERE THEY ARE.

WHY, YOU COMPLETELY MISLED ME. IT IS NO DRAGGING OR TUGGING CREATURE AS YOU'D HAVE ME BELIEVE.

IT'S A RIDER OF BEASTS! WE'D BETTER NOT STAY HERE!

AND THE THREE ANIMALS RAN AWAY AS FAST AS THEY COULD.

Readers' Choice

Counting Floors

Illustrations: Ram Waeerkar

Based on a story sent by T.S. Jyothi, Bombay

THE SCHOOL FOR **ORANGUTANS**

Script : Ashvin
Illustrations : J.P. Irani

THERE ARE FOUR TYPES OF APES. THE ORANGUTAN IS THE RAREST OF THEM. THERE ARE ONLY ABOUT 12,000 LEFT IN THE JUNGLES OF MALAYSIA AND INDONESIA. AND IF THEY ARE NOT TAKEN CARE OF, THERE IS A DANGER THAT THERE WILL BE NO ORANGUTANS LEFT IN THE WORLD IN A FEW YEARS.

HUNTERS CATCH THEM TO SELL. BUT ORANGUTANS GENERALLY DO NOT LIVE LONG WHEN TAKEN OUT OF THE JUNGLE. THEY DIE OF HUMAN DISEASES LIKE FLU, MALARIA AND TUBERCULOSIS.

MAN IS THE GREATEST ENEMY OF THESE GENTLE CREATURES. TRIBESMEN HUNT THEM FOR FOOD.

MALAYSIA AND INDONESIA HAVE PASSED A LAW FORBIDDING PEOPLE TO KEEP ORANGUTANS AS PETS. TAME ORANGUTANS ARE BEING RETURNED TO THE JUNGLE. BUT THIS IS NOT AN EASY TASK. THE ORANGUTANS PREFER TO STAY WITH HUMANS AND BEHAVE LIKE THEM. THE YOUNGER ONES DO NOT EVEN KNOW HOW TO CLIMB TREES.

THESE YOUNGSTERS ARE FIRST SENT TO A TRAINING CAMP. THERE THEY ARE TAUGHT HOW TO CLIMB TREES.

WHEN THEY'RE OLD ENOUGH, THEY ARE TAKEN TO A FOREST. THERE THEY ARE FORCED TO STAY IN THE TREES.
IF THEY ARE CAUGHT WALKING ON THE GROUND...

...THEY ARE SPANKED.

THEY ARE FED FROM PLATFORMS HIGH ABOVE THE GROUND.

AT THE END OF THE COURSE THE FEEDING IS STOPPED AND THE ORANGUTANS HAVE TO FIND THEIR OWN FOOD. THOSE WHO CAN FIND THEIR OWN FOOD ARE LEFT IN THE JUNGLE TO TAKE CARE OF THEMSELVES.

THE OTHERS ARE BROUGHT BACK TO THE TRAINING CAMP.
SEVERAL ORANGUTANS HAVE BEEN RETURNED TO THE JUNGLE IN THIS WAY.

THE SMART RUSE

Script : Rina Mukherji

Illustrations :
Ashok Dongre

?!

WHAT ARE YOU DOING IN MY HOUSE!

OAH...OAH...OAH ...OAAAAH!
WHAT'S THAT?
THE CUBS ARE CRYING.

WHY ARE THEY CRYING, WIFE?

THEY WANT FRESH TIGER MEAT. THEY WON'T TOUCH YESTERDAY'S LEFTOVERS.

THEY WON'T?
THEY EAT TIGERS!

THE TIGER RAN AWAY IN TERROR...

... AND THE JACKALS LIVED HAPPILY EVER AFTER IN THE TIGER'S DEN.
WON'T THE TIGER BE BACK, FATHER?
OH, NO, DEARS! HE IS TOO SCARED OF YOU!

TINKLE TRICKS & TREATS* TTT-40

A How many times would you write the digit 5 if you wrote down all numbers from 0 to 100?

B The following pictures are in sequence. The illustrator has not completed picture D. Can you?

A B C D

C One of these butterflies is slightly different from the others. Which one?

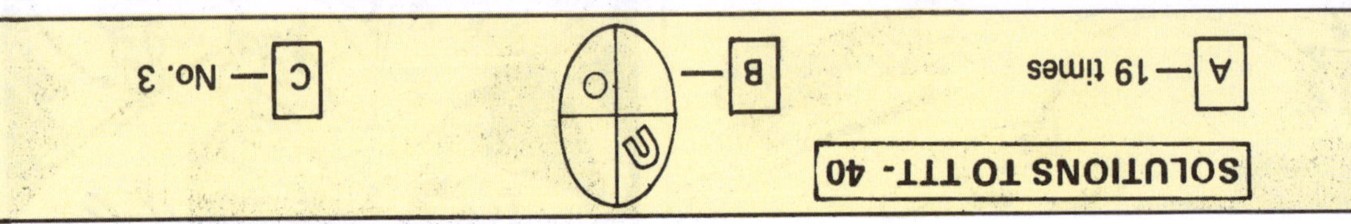

* Refer to the footnote under the Editor's Note

NO. 54
Rs. 3
TINKLE
AMAR CHITRA KATHA
THE FORTNIGHTLY
FOR CHILDREN
FROM THE HOUSE OF
AMAR CHITRA KATHA
THE SCHOOL
FOR ORANGUTANS
ASHOKA TREE
THE HURRICANE
THAT HID IN A TREE

ABOUT TANTRI THE MANTRI

If there's one word to describe the iconic Tantri the Mantri, it's evil. Tantri is an evil man, through and through. And yet, he's one of *Tinkle*'s most loved characters. There's something endearing about his perseverance and never-say-die attitude as he tries over and over again to get rid of Raja Hooja and become ruler of Hujli in his place.

Tantri's schemes have an almost 100 per cent failure rate. He has fallen off cliffs, tumbled into valleys, broken all bones in his body, had bombs explode in his face, been attacked by robots and had so many more unfortunate outcomes in his quest for power. The inventiveness of his various schemes and the comical backfires of each of them make Tantri a unique villain–one you wish you could be scared of but just can't help laughing at. Therein lies the genius of the character.

Tantri made his debut in *Tinkle* no. 51 in January 1984. His first adventure was scripted by veteran writer and editor, Mr. Prasad Iyer, and illustrated by the talented Mr. Ashok Dongre. While Tantri's character trajectory has been more or less constant, he has had various visual makeovers through the years. Several artists have worked on Tantri, from Mr. Anand Mande to Mr. Savio Mascarenhas (the current Art Director of *Tinkle* and *Amar Chitra Katha*). Finally in 2013 Mr. Vineet Nair inherited Tantri and he still illustrates the wily minister's woes and mishaps. Each artist presented their interpretation of Tantri. While Mr. Dongre depicted Tantri as a short, sharp-featured man, Mr. Mande drew him as a lanky, long-nosed figure. In charting the course of Tantri's evolution, one can witness the unique stamp each artist left on him, while retaining his endearing roguery.

Over the years, Tantri has found sympathizers and co-conspirators in the form of evil inventors (such as Dushtabuddhi) and assassins (such as DeadHit). He even has a witch named Hoki for a wife, although she does not partake in his schemes and doesn't approve of them either. With a widening cast of unique characters, Tantri's villainy has not been diluted but only strengthened. Now, if only Raja Hooja would be kind enough to buzz off and leave his throne for Tantri...

D

MULTIPLYING BY NINE

It's possible to multiply any number by 9 very quickly on your fingers.

Hold your fingers palm upwards and number each finger from 1 to 10 from left to right. Whichever number you wish to multiply by 9, bend down the finger bearing that number.

Then count how many fingers are left standing up on either side of the bent finger.

A. For example,to multiply 9 by 4, bend finger no. 4 and count the fingers to the left and to the right of it.
The answer is 3 and 6, i.e. 36

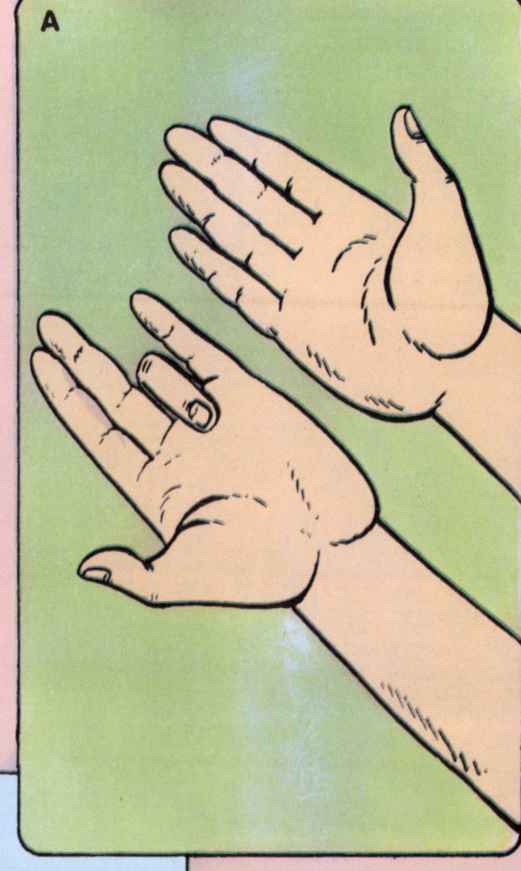

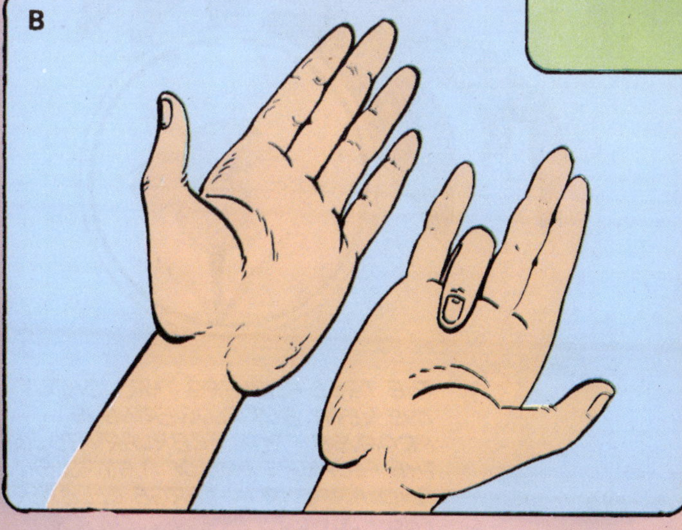

B. To multiply 9 by 7 bend down finger number 7 and you will see that the number is 6 and 3, i.e. 63.

ASHOKA TREE

Script: J.D. Isloor
Illustrations: Anand Mande

Raghu Based on an idea suggested by Nilotpal Brahma

*Readers Write...**

I am a regular reader of TINKLE. But since I stay in a hostel, I hardly get to read it as all the boys are anxious to see it!

S. B. Bijan, Pune

Why don't you start TINKLE Clubs all over the country so that readers can become members and get to know each other?

Varun Kapoor, New Delhi

(We hope to in the near future – Editor)

I hope you will never stop TINKLE and please give us some more features with more pages. I don't mind paying more!

Puneet Saim, Bombay

I am very fond of posters. Why don't you publish a poster and put it in TINKLE, at least once a month?

Shafeeq Qureshi, Kashmir

(We publish a wall paper – Amar India. I have sent you a complimentary copy – Editor)

Recently you have been publishing too many Readers' Choice stories. I would suggest that you restrict these to only one or at the most two in each issue. The rest should be your own.

Kapil Desai, Bombay

(We have found that our readers enjoy participating in TINKLE. They get a sense of belonging – Editor)

* Refer to the footnote under the Editor's Note

Mooshik Based on an idea suggested by Lloyd Bailey, Bombay

Mooshik
Based on an idea suggested by Rolando Fernandes, Goa

To Our Readers

TINKLE SUBSCRIPTIONS:
All new subscriptions and renewals of the old ones are accepted at:

PARTHA BOOKS DIVISION
Nav Prabhat Chambers, Ranade Road, Dadar, Bombay 400 028.
The annual subscription rate for 24 issues is Rs. 72/- per year (add Rs. 5/- on outstation cheques). Drafts/cheques/M.O. should be in favour of PARTHA BOOKS DIVISION.

While sending your subscription, mention your birthday, to receive a surprise gift from Uncle Pai.

Readers' Contributions should be addressed to Editor, TINKLE, Mahalaxmi Chambers (Basement), 22 Bhulabhai Desai Road, Bombay 400 026.

Readers' Choice:
* Please send only folktales you have heard and not those you have read in books, magazines or textbooks. Rs. 25/- will be paid for every accepted contribution.
* Send a self-addressed stamped envelope if you want the story to be returned.
* Please do not send photographs until asked for.

This happened to me:
You can write on your own strange, thrilling or amusing experience or adventure. Rs 15/- will be paid for every accepted contribution

Readers Write...
1. Mail your letters to: Tinkle. P. Bag No. 16541, Bombay 400 026.
2. Please give your address in your letters, if you want a reply.

TINKLE TRICKS AND TREATS
1. Mail your entry to: Tinkle Competition Section, P. Bag No. 16541, Bombay 400 026
2. The first 50 all-correct entries received by us will each win a **Flying Disc (Jr.)**, costing Rs 16
3. The next 50 all-correct entries received by us will each win a copy of the AMAR CHITRA KATHA title **The Bridegroom's Rings** (Issue dated April 1, 1984)

CUT HERE

ENTRY FORM*

NAME: ____________________

____

ADDRESS: ____________________

____

____

STATE: ____________________

____

PIN ☐☐☐☐☐☐

MY SOLUTIONS TTT- 40

A ____________________

B

C ____________________

* Refer to the footnote under the Editor's Note

THE DIVINE MANGO

Illustrations : Ashok Dongre

Readers' Choice

Based on a story sent by M.G. Sham Prashant, Bangalore

THE MERCHANT AND THE TAILOR

Script : Luis M. Fernandes

Illustrations : Ram Waeerkar

THE MERCHANT KEPT GOING BACK TO THE SHOP. TILL FINALLY—
I WANT TEN CAPS MADE OUT OT THAT CLOTH.
THEY'LL BE READY TOMORROW EVENING, SIR.

I'VE GOT THE BETTER OF HIM! I DON'T THINK MUCH CLOTH COULD BE LEFT OVER AFTER HE HAS MADE THOSE TEN CAPS.

AND NOW I CAN WEAR A NEW CAP EACH DAY FOR TEN DAYS.

ARE THE CAPS READY?
YES.

HERE YOU ARE, SIR.
WHAT?

YOU ASKED ME TO MAKE TEN CAPS OUT OF THAT PIECE OF CLOTH, SIR. HERE THEY ARE. NOW PLEASE PAY ME.

THE MERCHANT WENT AWAY A SADDER BUT WISER MAN.

OUR SOLAR SYSTEM—2

Script: J.D. Isloor
Illustrations:
Anand Mande

SATURN HAS AMAZING RINGS AROUND IT.
THE RINGS ARE THIN BANDS CONSISTING OF SWARMS OF ROCKY PARTICLES.
THE RINGS SEEN FROM VARIOUS ANGLES.
LATEST STUDIES HAVE SHOWN THAT URANUS TOO IS CIRCLED BY FAINT RINGS.
BUT NONE OF THE OTHER SEVEN PLANETS HAVE RINGS AROUND THEM.

SEEN FROM SPACE, THE EARTH APPEARS BLUE AND WHITE. THE BLUE COLOUR IS DUE TO THE FACT THAT MOST OF THE SURFACE OF THE EARTH IS COVERED BY WATER. THE WHITE IS DUE TO THE CLOUDS ABOVE THE EARTH.

MARS IS SOMETIMES CALLED THE RED PLANET. THE RED COLOUR OF ITS SURFACE IS CAUSED BY LARGE AMOUNTS OF IRON OXIDE.

JUPITER HAS A GREAT RED SPOT. THE RED SPOT IS A PERMANENTLY SPINNING WHIRLPOOL OF CLOUD.

NEPTUNE AND URANUS ARE GREENISH IN COLOUR.
IT IS BELIEVED THAT BOTH PLANETS HAVE ROCKY CENTRES COATED WITH ICE.

THE COLDEST...

PLUTO BEING FARTHEST FROM THE SUN IS THE COLDEST PLANET. IT IS SO COLD THAT AIR OF THE KIND WE BREATHE WOULD TURN INTO A LIQUID THERE.

...AND THE HOTTEST

MERCURY IS CLOSEST TO THE SUN. BUT IT IS NOT THE HOTTEST PLANET. THE HOTTEST IS VENUS.
VENUS HAS THICK CLOUDS AROUND IT AND THESE CLOUDS PREVENT HEAT FROM ESCAPING FROM THE SURFACE.
THE SURFACE TEMPERATURE ON VENUS IS OVER 400°C. HOT ENOUGH TO MELT LEAD !

RESULTS OF THE COMPLETE-THE-STORY COMPETITION No. 8*

We were happy to find that many TINKLE readers participated in the competition this time. We were faced with a number of imaginative entries which made our task of awarding prizes a difficult one !

The prize-winning entry :

When the three men heard the knocks on the door, two of them quickly hid under a bed. The other, who was a little braver, went to the window and looked out. There he saw a tiger standing on two legs. He knew at once that this must be a man in the disguise of a tiger. He went back to tell his friends who came out from under the bed. They opened the door and all three of them pounced on the so-called tiger. They dragged him to the home of the village chieftain. But the chief was not at home, so they decided to pull off the disguise themselves and unmask the man. Imagine their surprise whan they saw that it was none other than the village chieftain who was masquerading as a tiger ! The chief begged their forgiveness, but by that time all the villagers had gathered. When they were told the whole story, they decided to banish the chief from their village immediately. They made the brave man the new village chieftain.

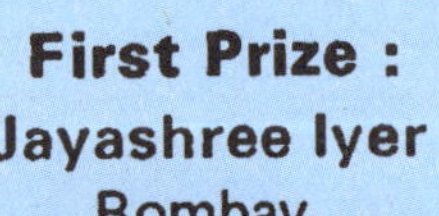

First Prize :
Jayashree Iyer
Bombay

Consolation Prizes :
A consolation prize of Rs. 25/- each has been awarded to **Rajasri Mohan** of Hubli and **Anil George** of Bombay

* Refer to the footnote under the Editor's Note

Kalia
THE CROW
Script:
LUIS
Illustrations:
RAM WAEERKAR

IT'S SO COOL AND PLEASANT HERE!
LET'S SLEEP FOR A WHILE.

IS IT SAFE?
OH, YES! I MAY BE SMALL BUT EVERYBODY IS AFRAID OF ME.

EVEN LIONS AND TIGERS AND...
SPLAT

YOU STUPID BIRD!

FLY AWAY BEFORE I...!

SPLAT

KNOCK HIM DOWN FROM THERE, DOOB DOOB.
CERTAINLY!

ER... HOW DO I DO THAT?
HIT THE TREE WITH YOUR TAIL.

NOBODY CAN DROP ROTTEN FRUITS ON ME AND GET AWAY WITH IT!

WHAM

GET UP, CHAMATAKA! GET UP!

I'LL TAKE HIM TO THE RIVER AND THROW SOME WATER ON HIM.

OOOOH... OHH... WHAT HAPPENED?
HE IS COMING ROUND.

ER... CHAMATAKA, I HOPE YOU ARE ALL RIGHT.

A BRANCH FELL ON YOU AND...
HIDE, QUICKLY!

THERE'S A DEER COMING THIS WAY.

LOOK OUT! THERE'S DANGER HERE!

IT'S KALIA! AGAIN!

I'LL KNOCK HIM DOWN FROM THERE.
I'LL CATCH THAT DEER, YET.

THUCK
OH, NO!

ANYWAY, I WON'T HAVE THE TROUBLE OF TAKING HIM TO THE RIVER THIS TIME!

Readers' Choice

THE ADVENTURES OF SUPPANDI - 6

Illustrations : Ram Waeerkar

Based on a story sent by A. Murlidhar, Hyderabad

HE COUNTED BEFORE EATING

A folktale from Goa

Script:
Luis M. Fernandes

Illustrations:
Ram Waeerkar

SOANSOANA

...SOANSOANNNN!
THAT'S FOUR.

THE SON-IN-LAW DID NOT KNOW THAT HE WAS COUNTING EACH PANCAKE TWICE. AND FINALLY—
THEY HAVE MADE TEN. WONDERFUL!

AT TEA-TIME, HIS WIFE'S BROTHER RUSHED IN TO GRAB A PANCAKE, BUT—
NOT NOW, PEDRO! LET YOUR BROTHER-IN-LAW EAT FIRST.

GO AND CALL HIM FOR TEA.

THE SON-IN-LAW CAME EAGERLY TO THE TABLE...

...AND BEGAN TO EAT.
DELICIOUS!

WHILE THE LITTLE BOY WATCHED FROM THE DOORWAY—
THAT'S ONE.

THAT'S TWO!

MOTHER, MOTHER HE HAS EATEN TWO!
NEVER MIND! THERE ARE STILL THREE LEFT.

MOTHER HE HAS EATEN ANOTHER ONE!
WELL, THERE ARE STILL TWO LEFT.

MOTHER!

HE HAS EATEN THE FOURTH ONE!
HE HAS?!

WELL, ONE IS ENOUGH FOR YOU.
MOTHER!

HE IS EATING THE FIFTH ONE TOO!
OH!

IT'S A GOOD THING I COUNTED HOW MANY THEY MADE OR I WOULD NEVER HAVE DARED TO EAT FIVE WHOLE PANCAKES!

Illustrations:
Ashok Dongre

...TILL IT MET A HARE.
OH, SWEET LITTLE BUN, I'LL EAT YOU UP!
DON'T EAT ME, DEAR LITTLE HARE. I'LL SING YOU A SONG.

DUM-DEE-DUM-DEE... DUM...

HEY!
...DUM -DUM-DUM...

THE BUN GOT AWAY FROM THE HARE AND ROLLED ON AND ON. SUDDENLY-
A WOLF!

PLEASE DON'T EAT ME UP, SIR! I'LL SING A SONG FOR YOU.

DUM-DEE -DUM-DEE-DUM...

!
...DUM -DUM -DUM!

A LITTLE LATER-
STOP FOR ME, O LITTLE BROWN BUN. I WANT TO EAT YOU UP.

BUT THE BUN GOT AWAY FROM THE BEAR, TOO.
COME BACK!
...DUM -DUM-DUM...

... DUM-DUM...
OH-OH, A FOX!

GOOD MORNING, LITTLE BUN. I'M GOING TO EAT YOU UP!
LET ME SING FOR YOU FIRST.

DUM-DEE...
I CAN'T HEAR YOU.

WILL YOU SIT ON MY SNOUT AND SING AGAIN?
ALL RIGHT.

DUM-DEE...
I STILL CAN'T HEAR YOU.

PLEASE SIT ON MY TONGUE.

...AND SING AGAIN, FOR THE LAST TIME.
ALL RIGHT.

BUT AS SOON AS THE BUN ROLLED DOWN TO HIS TONGUE...
DUM DEE DUM

...THE FOX GOBBLED IT UP.
AND THAT REALLY WAS THE LAST TIME THE BUN SANG.

AFTER POLLINATION

Illustrations: Anand Mande

WHEN POLLEN GRAINS REACH A PISTIL OF THE SAME KIND OF FLOWER, THEY GROW A LONG TUBE. THE TUBE GROWS DOWNWARDS INTO THE PISTIL UNTIL IT REACHES AN OVULE IN THE OVARY.
THE OVULE CAN NOW DEVELOP INTO A SEED.
EACH OF THE OVULES BECOMES A SEED IN THIS WAY.

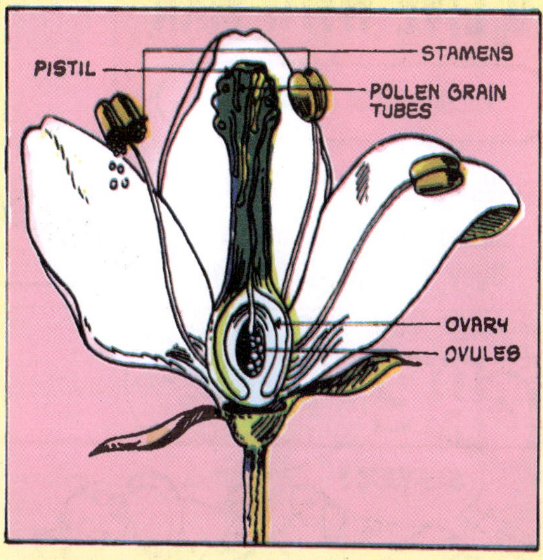

HOW THE APPLE FLOWER BECOMES A FRUIT.

MEANWHILE, THE STAMENS AND PART OF THE PISTIL DRY UP.
THE PETALS TOO FALL OFF.
THE OVARY OF THE FLOWER OFTEN STORES FOOD AROUND THE SEED OR SEEDS.
WITH SEEDS AND STORED FOOD THE OVARY IS CALLED A FRUIT.

A FRUIT MAY HAVE ONLY ONE SEED OR SEVERAL SEEDS.
A TOMATO FOR EXAMPLE HAS SEVERAL SEEDS.
SO TOO, BEANS AND PUMPKINS.
A MANGO, ON THE OTHER HAND HAS ONLY ONE SEED.

HOW THE CAT CAME TO LIVE WITH MAN

READERS' CHOICE

Illustrations : V.B. Halbe

Based on a story sent by Bijoy S. Singh, Dehradun

I'VE FINISHED, SISTER – CLEAR ALL THIS AWAY.
YES, BROTHER.

AS USUAL, THERE'S NOT A MORSEL LEFT FOR ME.

ONE DAY, THE TIGER FELL ILL AND MANY ANIMALS CAME TO SEE HIM.

THE CAT SPOKE A FEW WORDS TO EVERYONE, MAKING THE GUESTS FEEL WELCOME AND COMFORTABLE.

BUT JUST THEN—
SISTER! LIGHT THE HOOKAH AND PASS IT AROUND. GO AND BE QUICK ABOUT IT!

BROTHER, THERE IS NO FIRE IN THE HOUSE.
THEN GO AND GET A FIREBRAND FROM THE DWELLINGS OF MEN. RUN!

SO THE CAT RAN, OVER STONES AND TWIGS AND TWIGS AND STONES...

...TO THE VILLAGE. THERE—
LOOK! WHAT A SWEET FURRY THING!

DON'T BE AFRAID. WE WON'T HURT YOU.

SHE'S SO SOFT AND SILKY!
PURR... PURRR... NOBODY EVER MADE ME FEEL SO HAPPY!
AND FORGETTING ALL ABOUT THE ERRAND SHE HAD COME ON, THE CAT LET THE CHILDREN CUDDLE AND PET HER FOR A LONG TIME.

SUDDENLY, THE JUNGLE SHOOK WITH A THUNDEROUS SOUND—
GRA-OWR!

IT WAS THE TIGER!
OH, NO! THE FIREBRAND! HOW COULD I HAVE FORGOTTEN ABOUT IT? HOW COULD I?

THE CAT RAN INTO A HOUSE, PICKED UP A FIREBRAND...

AND RAN BACK, OVER TWIGS AND STONES AND STONES AND TWIGS...

...SUDDENLY AGAIN CAME THAT LOUD ROAR...
RRRROWR!

...AND THE TREMBLING CAT LOOKED UP INTO THE PURPLE, RED-EYED FACE OF THE TIGER.

SO FRIGHTENED WAS SHE, THAT SHE DROPPED THE FIREBRAND AT HIS FEET...

...AND SCAMPERED BACK TO THE VILLAGE.
LOOK— THE CAT HAS COME BACK.

IT MUST HAVE BEEN THE TIGER WHO SCARED HER SO MUCH.
YES, STAY WITH US, LITTLE ONE. DON'T GO BACK.

YOU WON'T, WILL YOU?
I WON'T. NEVER.

AND THAT IS HOW CATS CAME TO LIVE WITH MEN.

WEATHER AND CLIMATE

Script : J. D. Isloor

Illustrations : Anand Mande

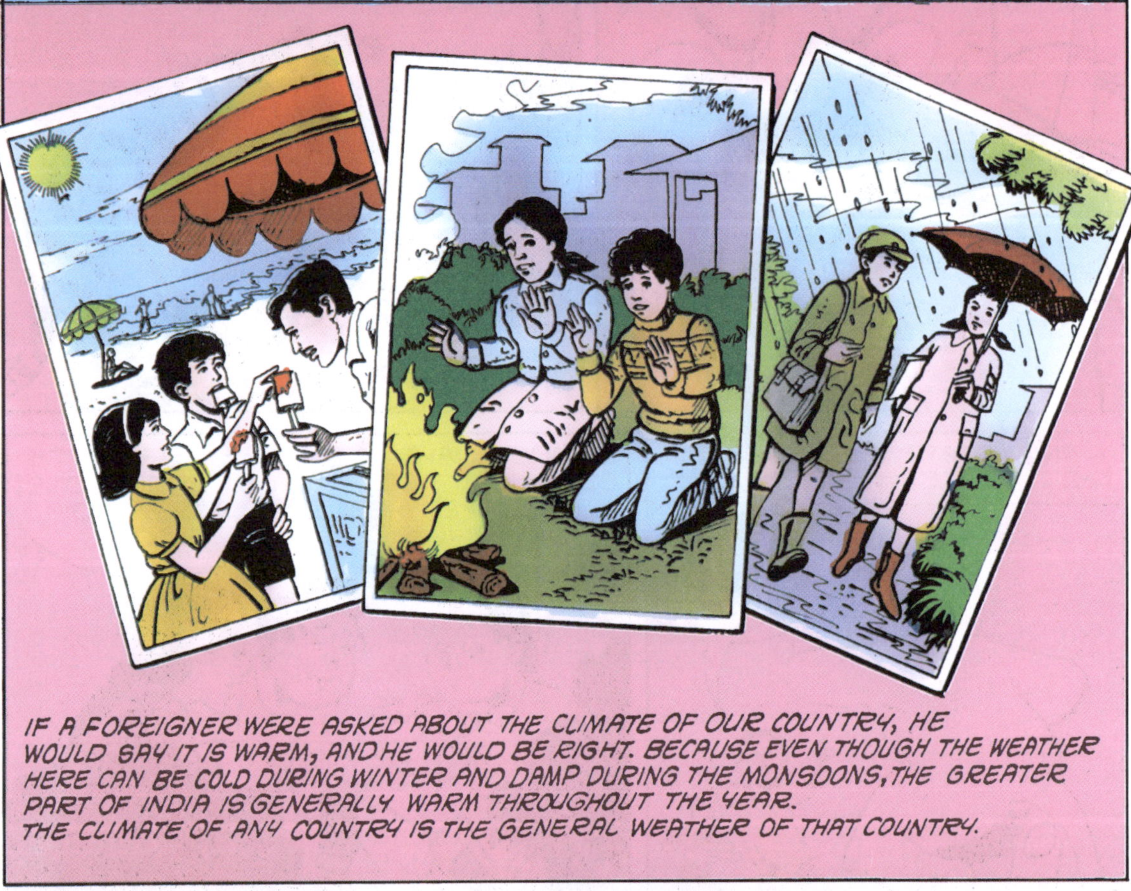

IF A FOREIGNER WERE ASKED ABOUT THE CLIMATE OF OUR COUNTRY, HE WOULD SAY IT IS WARM, AND HE WOULD BE RIGHT. BECAUSE EVEN THOUGH THE WEATHER HERE CAN BE COLD DURING WINTER AND DAMP DURING THE MONSOONS, THE GREATER PART OF INDIA IS GENERALLY WARM THROUGHOUT THE YEAR.
THE CLIMATE OF ANY COUNTRY IS THE GENERAL WEATHER OF THAT COUNTRY.

EUROPEANS LIVE DIFFERENTLY.
THE SUN SHINES MILDLY ON THEIR COUNTRIES. AND THE WINTERS ARE LONG. SO THEIR HOUSES HAVE TO BE ARTIFICIALLY HEATED. AND THEIR CLOTHING IS HEAVY AND WARM. MEAT IS AN IMPORTANT PART OF THEIR DIET.

ESKIMOS LIVE IN A STILL COLDER CLIMATE. THEIR HOUSES (IGLOOS) ARE BUILT OUT OF SNOW. AS CROPS CANNOT GROW ON THEIR LAND, THE ESKIMOS LIVE MAINLY ON FOOD FROM THE SEA INCLUDING FISH AND SEALS. THEIR CLOTHING IS MADE OUT OF ANIMAL SKINS.

THE CHIEF FACTOR IN CLIMATE IS THE AMOUNT OF HEAT RECEIVED FROM THE SUN. THE EARTH IS SURROUNDED BY THE LAYER OF GAS THAT WE BREATHE AND WHICH WE CALL THE ATMOSPHERE. BEFORE SUNLIGHT REACHES THE SURFACE OF THE EARTH, IT HAS TO PASS THROUGH THE ATMOSPHERE WHICH REFLECTS ABOUT HALF THE HEAT BACK INTO SPACE.

BECAUSE OF THE CURVATURE OF THE EARTH, THE RAYS OF THE SUN HIT THE EARTH AT DIFFERENT ANGLES.
THE RAYS ARE DIRECT AT THE EQUATOR. SO THIS IS THE HOTTEST REGION. AT THE POLES A SIMILAR AMOUNT OF RAYS SPREAD OVER A LARGER DISTANCE. SO THIS REGION RECEIVES MUCH LESS HEAT.

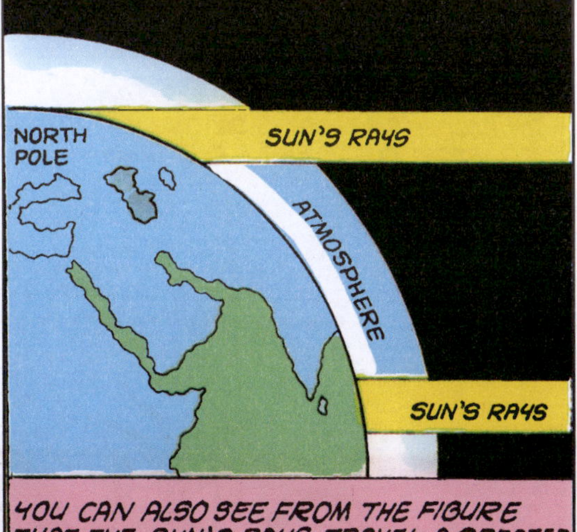

YOU CAN ALSO SEE FROM THE FIGURE THAT THE SUN'S RAYS TRAVEL A GREATER DISTANCE THROUGH THE ATMOSPHERE AT THE POLAR REGION THAN AT THE EQUATOR. BECAUSE OF THIS, THE RAYS LOSE A LOT OF HEAT BEFORE THEY REACH THE GROUND AT THE POLES.

OCEANS ALSO CONTRIBUTE TO THE CLIMATE OF A PLACE. LAND HEATS UP FASTER THAN WATER. LAND COOLS FASTER TOO. LONG AFTER THE LAND HAS COOLED THE WATER IS STILL VERY WARM. THIS IS WHY, IN WINTER, PLACES NEAR THE SEA, LIKE BOMBAY AND GOA ARE MUCH WARMER THAN PLACES IN THE INTERIOR LIKE NAGPUR AND AHMEDABAD.

IN SUMMER, THE HOT SUN QUICKLY HEATS UP THE LAND BUT THE WATER OF THE OCEAN TAKES TIME TO GET HEATED. AS A RESULT THE SEA IS COOLER THAN THE LAND AND PLACES NEAR THE SEA ARE COOLER THAN PLACES IN THE INTERIOR.

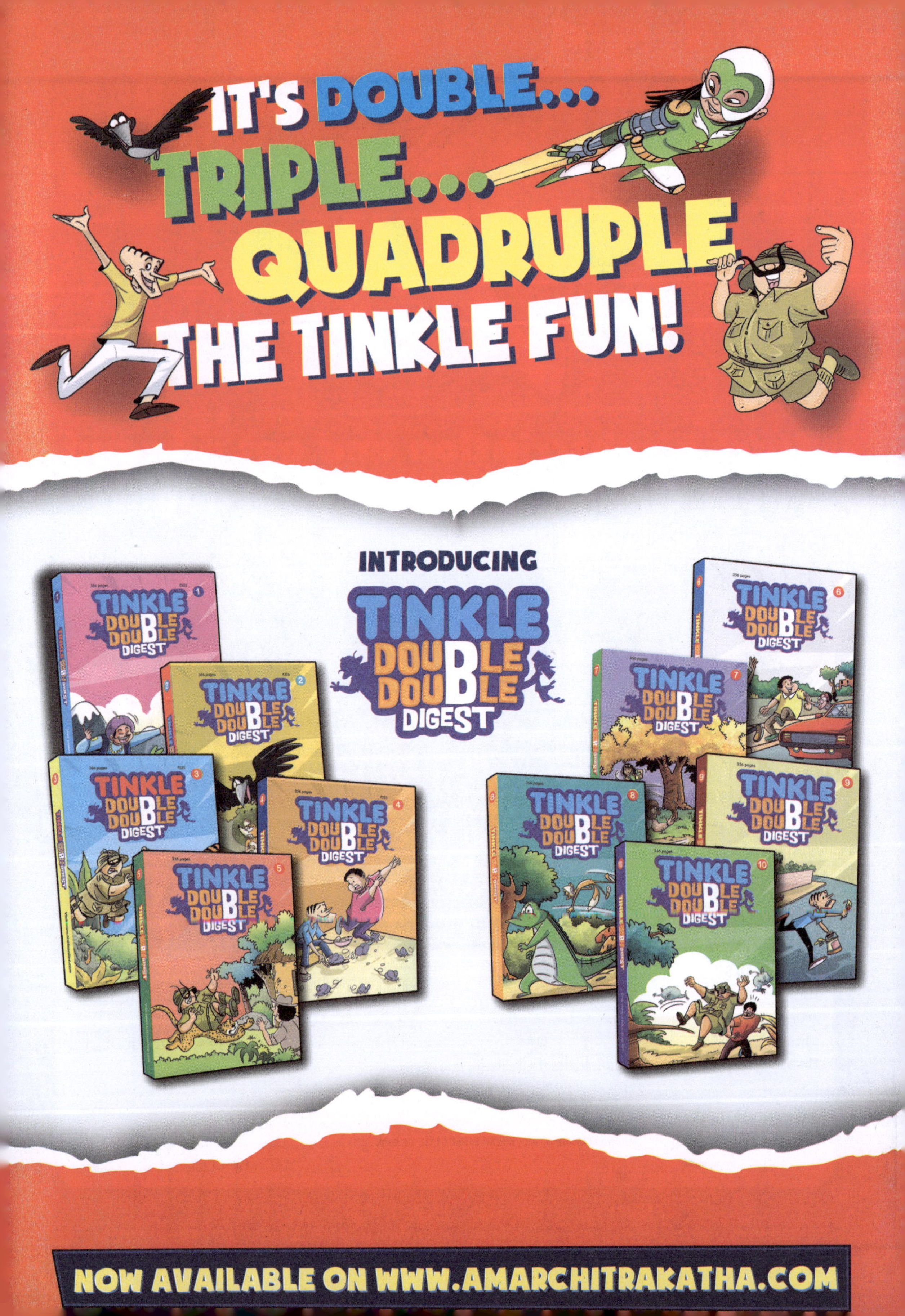

IT'S DOUBLE...
TRIPLE...
QUADRUPLE
THE TINKLE FUN!